SEP 03 2014

7628 3029

273926

29

D0167647

SPECIAL MESSAGE TO READERS

THE ULVERSCROFT FOUNDATION
(registered UK charity number 264873)
was established in 1972 to provide funds for
research, diagnosis and treatment of eye diseases.
Examples of major projects funded by
the Ulverscroft Foundation are:-

* The Children's Eye Unit at Moorfields Eye
  Hospital, London
* The Ulverscroft Children's Eye Unit at Great
  Ormond Street Hospital for Sick Children
* Funding research into eye diseases and
  treatment at the Department of Ophthalmology,
  University of Leicester
* The Ulverscroft Vision Research Group,
  Institute of Child Health
* Twin operating theatres at the Western
  Ophthalmic Hospital, London
* The Chair of Ophthalmology at the Royal
  Australian College of Ophthalmologists

You can help further the work of the Foundation
by making a donation or leaving a legacy.
Every contribution is gratefully received. If you
would like to help support the Foundation or
require further information, please contact:

THE ULVERSCROFT FOUNDATION
The Green, Bradgate Road, Anstey
Leicester LE7 7FU, England
Tel: (0116) 236 4325

website: www.foundation.ulverscroft.com

NONE BUT HE

When Mandy's boyfriend dies in a motorbike accident, she is left alone with a young child and little money. So when her son's uncle Jon offers her a job as his receptionist — as well as a home with himself and his beautiful but spoilt wife, Gillian — she gratefully accepts. But Mandy soon becomes aware of Jon's unhappiness, as well as her own growing love for him. Perhaps if she accepts the attentions of Mike Sinclair, an attractive Irish bachelor, it will help her to keep her true feelings hidden . . .

PATRICIA ROBINS

NONE BUT HE

Complete and Unabridged

LINFORD
Leicester

First published in Great Britain in 1973 by
Hurst & Blackett Ltd

First Linford Edition
published 2014

Copyright © 1973 by Patricia Robins
All rights reserved

A catalogue record for this book is available
from the British Library.

ISBN 978–1–4448–2047–8

Published by
F. A. Thorpe (Publishing)
Anstey, Leicestershire

Set by Words & Graphics Ltd.
Anstey, Leicestershire
Printed and bound in Great Britain by
T. J. International Ltd., Padstow, Cornwall

This book is printed on acid-free paper

1

Mandy peered at her reflection in the dressing table mirror and gave a helpless little shrug. She was losing her looks and at the age of twenty, she told herself wryly, she was a little on the young side to be doing so.

She turned away from the mirror and slipped a loose shirt over her pink trousers. The folds of material hid her thinness the way she had once worn it to hide her bulk. Now Jon would not be so likely to notice the loss of weight. She was not so confident that Gillian's sharp eyes would miss the truth. But then Gillian wouldn't care how thin she was, so it did not matter.

The girl turned back to the mirror and began to apply mascara to her lashes. Although her own were thick and curling and the grey-green eyes were beautiful enough without any aids.

1

They looked enormous in her chalk-white angular little face.

In the bedroom next door her kindly landlady was putting Timmy to bed. She could hear the baby's cheerful gurgles and Mrs Phillips' loud but affectionate voice as she settled the little boy for the night. All was well, Mandy told herself with a sigh of relief. Timmy wasn't used to being put to bed by anyone other than herself and she did not want to go out to dinner leaving behind a screaming fractious child for her landlady to baby-mind. She was immensely grateful to Mrs Phillips for offering to look after Timmy; this despite her firm ruling when Mandy had moved in that the modest rental did not and would not include a baby-minding service.

As Mandy reached for her jacket her wide soft mouth curved suddenly into a mischievous grin. The apparently stern and unbending north country woman was weakening day by day beneath the onslaught of her little boy's charm.

Though Mrs Phillips would die rather than admit it, Mandy was certain that she was really thrilled to have Timmy all to herself this evening. No doubt once Mandy was out of the house, she would relax that outward rigid indifference and perhaps even kiss the baby good night!

It had been agreed between them that Mandy should slip out of the house when she was dressed without looking in on Timmy lest her appearance and impending departure should upset him.

'I'll take your good night and thank you as said!' had been Mrs Phillips' matter-of-fact comment as she carried Timmy off for his bath. 'Have a good time!' she added, almost as if this wish was against her better nature rather than because of it. It was part of her policy as far as Mandy was concerned to maintain a haughty disapproval of everything about her — the way she dressed, the way she behaved, the way she thought. Most of all, she made it quite clear that she disapproved violently of Mandy's illegitimate child. She had only relented and taken Mandy and Timmy in as lodgers because, she had explained, Timmy's father would have made a decent woman, an honest woman, of Mandy had he lived. It wasn't Mandy's fault he'd had that fatal motor-bike accident, though, mind you, it was Mandy's fault and no other's that she'd been pregnant at the time.

Desperate for somewhere to live with her baby, Mandy shut her ears to the moralising lectures and obvious disapproval, grateful to have a roof over her head at a rent she could afford and near enough to her work and a day nursery for Timmy. She'd walked miles, knocked on door after door, only to be met with 'No vacancy' as soon as the landlady saw the pram and her ringless finger. She'd been close to giving up the whole unequal struggle of trying to keep her baby that afternoon she'd knocked on Mrs Phillips' door. Now, almost a year later, she was beginning to realise that a heart of gold was encased in that angular upright figure and that behind the stern disapproving exterior there was an unwilling liking, if not admiration, for her in her efforts to do her best for the baby she had never meant to have but who now mattered more to her than anything or anyone in the world.

Mandy closed the front door behind her and, shivering in the cold darkness of the November night, walked hurriedly down to the bus stop. Jon and Gillian were staying in the better part of the town at the only really good hotel — the Manor. They were stopping over on their way to London, Jon had said on the telephone, and wanted her to dine with them. Before he left next morning he wanted to see Timmy. He hadn't seen him since that day in the mothers' and babies' home when he was three weeks old. Mandy remembered that afternoon as clearly as if it were through a huge magnifying glass.

Gillian had been there, tall, languid, beautiful Gillian, saying in that hard high voice of hers:

'But you must be out of your mind, Mandy. You'll ruin your life, you know. You're hardly likely to get married with a child hanging round your neck. Besides, it isn't fair to the kid. You ought to have it adopted.'

Jon had tried to stop the battering of words coming from his young wife's lips.

'Mandy has made up her mind, Gilly. It isn't for us to interfere. Anyway, I think she's right!'

How grateful she had been for those few added words! All the days of indecision, of trying to make up her mind what would be best for the tiny baby she loved so passionately and wanted to keep, had taken as much toll of her strength as the birth itself and the months of worry preceding it.

'You'll never manage!' Gillian had said, shrugging.

'I can try!' Mandy had flashed back.

'Other girls have managed. I want to keep him. He's mine and I love him!'

Jon had put a hand on her shoulder — a strangely warm comforting hand giving her faith in herself, in her future.

'We'll help, of course!' he said quietly. 'I'm afraid Pete didn't leave any money but I'll arrange an allowance of some sort.'

Gillian's voice, sharper than ever, had broken in.

'Mandy said she could manage, so why not let her see if she can. You'll only be propping up a . . . '

'Stop it, Gilly! It's my brother's child and I intend to help when and where I can.'

Near to tears, Mandy had said proudly:

'I don't need money, thank you, Jon. If I do, I'll ask for it, but I don't need . . . I don't *want* an allowance from you!'

Of course it wasn't true, but knowing how Gillian resented Jon's offer, she could not and would not take help until she was desperate. Although he said nothing at the time, she was sure Jon understood her desire for independence; recognised her need to keep her self-respect when she had so little of it left.

Unknown to Gillian, Mandy was certain, he'd sent a very generous cheque for Timmy's christening present. There'd been another substantial cheque and a box full of quite unsuitable, extravagant toys for Christmas and again on Timmy's birthday. With them had been a note saying:

I'd prefer you didn't write and thank me.

I'll take it as said. Love, Jon

Reading between the lines, Mandy guessed he did not want Gillian to know what he had done.

Now he had come to see his little nephew and Mandy was touched by his desire to do so. As a highly respectable young G.P. living a conventional life amongst conventional people, he could have been excused for not wanting to

8

know his brother's illegitimate child.

Mandy was so lost in thought she nearly passed the Manor Hotel. She stood for a moment outside, feeling suddenly terribly alone and uncertain. It was almost two years since she had been out anywhere at all, let alone to dinner in a smart hotel like the Manor. She'd forgotten how to behave, what aperitif to order before the meal if Jon offered her one; whether he would consult her about wine and if it were red with white meat or the other way round. Suddenly, her pink trousers and shirt felt all wrong, too way-out, too casual. Gillian, as always, would be incredibly smart, right up-to-date and very beautiful. Beside her, Mandy would feel *ingénue*, even gauche and ridiculous.

She felt like turning on her heel and running back to the comforting severity of Mrs Phillips' boarding house but at the same time, she knew her friend, Fiona, had been perfectly right when she said:

'Of course you'll go out to dinner, you stupid goof. You're in a rut, Mandy, and if you aren't careful, you'll settle into it for life. Here you are, offered some super free nosh and drinks at the best hotel and on the brink of saying you can't leave Timmy. Mrs Phillips can look after him. You haven't had a night out since the day you came here and that's a crime, not a virtue.'

Mandy had tried to argue.

'You don't know Gillian. She doesn't approve of me and . . . '

'And nothing!' Fiona had interrupted brashly. 'You say Jon is kind and nice and *he* invited you, not her. Don't be such a goof. Go!'

Smiling at the memory of Fiona's furious freckled face, the intensity with which she spoke, Mandy regained some of her courage. She pushed open the door of the hotel and, head high, walked into the lobby.

Almost before she had accustomed her eyes to the bright lights, Jon's tall rugged frame was towering over her, his

10

voice saying warm, welcoming things, his hand resting lightly on her arm as he drew her towards the lounge.

'Gilly's not quite ready; she'll be down presently. We'll have a drink in here. What do you feel like? Sherry? Gin and something?'

She felt herself relax. With Jon around she had nothing to be nervous about. She sat down in the deep comfortable armchair and looked up at him, knowing that the sight of him would hurt. He was so breath-takingly like Timmy's father, his younger brother whom she had loved so desperately and so briefly before he'd died. They had the same dark brown eyes beneath the same broad high forehead. Only their mouths were different, Jon's wide and straight and serious where Pete's had been upturned and full of daredevil mischief. Though four years separated them in age, the brothers had been very close, despite their opposite temperaments and ways of life. Jon had chosen the conventional life of a doctor, worked his way

11

steadily through medical school and qualified without difficulty. Pete had been unable to settle to anything after he left school, playing in a pop group, leaving it to hitch-hike round Europe and finally getting a job at a garage where he could indulge his passion for motor-bikes and speed. It was there he had met Mandy, a newly fledged secretary in her first job with the manager of the garage. They'd had a brief crazy courtship in which Pete had pursued her with all his charm and won her heart. She had known he was irresponsible, unlikely to be faithful, living for the mood of the moment, feckless even, but she'd loved him and had soon stopped caring about tomorrow in the first wild delight of newly found love. It was her first affair and she had been as uncaring as Pete about tomorrow. Nothing mattered but today — not even the alienation from her parents who wanted nothing more to do with her when they discovered she had been sleeping with Pete. She'd moved into Pete's minuscule flat and for a few glorious months she stopped thinking.

Then Pete was killed. She was so desolate she finally got in touch with her mother and was on the point of returning home, the prodigal daughter, when she realised she was pregnant. At first she was terrified; then with the thought that she still had a tiny part of Pete left to live for, her despair gave way to hope and even to a confused happiness. She found another job where she wasn't known, moved into a flat with two other girls and waited for the months to pass before she could hold Pete's baby in her arms. Neither her mother's written exhortations to have the baby adopted, nor her flatmate's efforts to persuade her to have an abortion, affected her in the least. But it was different when the child was finally born. She loved him desperately and once the idea was put in her head that he might have a better life if he were adopted, she lost her confidence and her assurance. She nursed him and watched the other girls the day their babies were removed for adoption, knowing she could never let Timmy go, but feeling she ought to. It was Matron who finally gave her back her will to keep him.

'He's yours, my dear, and if you feel strong enough to cope with all the difficulties I've pointed out to you, then you hang on to him. You're pretty, young, and a good girl despite what's happened to you. Some young man is going to find that out and want to marry you. Then your Timmy will have a father as well as a mother. Don't let anyone persuade you to part with him if you want to keep him.'

So she had kept him, despite that painful visit from Jon and Gillian — the first time she had met them and, she supposed, the last. She had not expected Pete's family to approve any more than her own.

Jon returned to the table carrying the sherry she had asked for and a glass of beer for himself. He smiled at her as he handed the glass to her and said:

'You're looking very pretty, Mandy. How's the boy?'

Mandy's face lit up.

'He's beautiful. At least, I think so!' she added quickly, afraid lest she should start boasting and boring Jon, who no doubt was only asking out of politeness. But when she remained silent he said:

'Well, tell me about him. How big is he now? Is he like Pete? Or you?'

Question and answer flowed quickly from one to the other. Jon seemed genuinely interested and was on the point of saying how much he was longing to meet his little nephew in the morning when Gillian interrupted. Her arrival had been unnoticed by either of them.

'I suppose you are going to offer me a seat and a drink?'

Jon sprang to his feet and Mandy at once noticed the taut expression on his face — as if he were keeping himself strictly under control.

'Sorry, darling!' he apologised. 'We

15

were so engrossed I never saw you come in. You look stunning, Gilly. Now, what will it be? Gin and Martini?'

Mandy felt herself relax as Gillian's face lost its look of irritation. Jon's compliment had done the trick and, Mandy thought, it was justified. Gillian did look stunning. Tall, dark, her beautiful figure outlined by the skin-tight jersey dress, Jon's young wife might have stepped off the cover of *Vogue*. She had, in point of fact, been a model before she married Jon three years ago. The beautiful way in which she held her head, the skilful way in which she had made up her face to show off the delicate bone structure, all bespoke the trained model, as did her walk and her posture. She was the perfect complement for Jon's rugged masculinity.

Whilst Jon was calling over a waiter to order Gillian's drink, Mandy found herself wondering what kind of a marriage this was. Jon was clearly in love with his beautiful wife. But what of

Gillian? Was she capable of loving anyone but herself? Somehow Mandy doubted it. She had disliked Gillian instinctively at their first meeting, aware she had nothing in common with the older girl. She had met girls like Gillian at the secretarial college, vain, self-opinionated and selfish. They were mostly highly ambitious and Mandy wondered now what had made Gillian marry Jon. Although he had a secure job for life, for many years to come there wouldn't be much of a life of luxury for the wife of a struggling young G.P. Perhaps Gillian had money of her own. Or perhaps Mandy was misjudging her and she had genuinely fallen in love with Jon. It wasn't so difficult to conceive. Jon was very attractive. If he lacked Pete's carefree gaiety and fun, he made up for it with a warm sensitivity she was beginning to appreciate.

Jon had been lighting a cigarette for Gillian. Now he turned back to Mandy to resume their conversation where it had broken off. He had barely mentioned Timmy's day nursery before Gillian's voice cut in:

'We're not going to have baby-talk all evening, are we? I'm sure Mandy would like a break from nurseries and nappies and I certainly would!'

For a split second Mandy thought Jon was going to say something violent. His face was red and his eyes were narrowed and angry. But he managed to control his anger and only a hint of it remained in his voice as he said:

'This is Mandy's evening, Gilly. And mine. I want to hear about the child.'

Gillian gave a disdainful shrug.

'Okay, okay. Don't blow your top, darling!' she said casually, although there was an edge to her voice which made Mandy feel acutely uncomfortable. Quickly she broke in:

'Gillian's quite right. I have more than enough of Timmy. Tell me about yourselves. How's the practice? Do you like living in Surrey?'

'It's a bit dull for Gilly,' Jon said.

'She'd like to get back to London but I'm afraid that's out of the question for a few years yet.'

'Dull is hardly the word!' Gillian added. 'Jon's tied to those ghastly surgery hours and we practically never get a dinner party organised without him being called out by some idiotic mother panicking over her offspring. I can tell you this much, Mandy — a G.P. doesn't have a life of his own. *Never* marry a doctor, my dear, because you come a very poor second to his work.'

Jon made no comment. He looked suddenly defeated, miserable; and Mandy felt a wave of sympathy for him. Even if Gillian were speaking the truth, it was a disloyalty to voice such views in public.

'I suppose you get involved in Jon's work, too,' she said placatingly. 'Answering phones and that kind of thing.'

'Not on your life!' Gillian retorted frankly. 'I'm absolutely hopeless with things like that. Jon has a secretary-nurse female, madly efficient, who copes far better than I could.'

'Then how do you fill your day?' Mandy asked curiously. Gillian didn't seem the type to be busy cooking or making curtains.

'You may well ask!' Gillian replied. 'I was busy enough when we moved house, getting that dreary old villa looking something like a real home. I despaired of doing so at one time, but I must say it looks reasonable now, though it took me ages and cost a fortune.'

'Gilly has made it beautiful!' Jon said quietly. 'You must come and see it one day soon, Mandy.'

The bored expression that had lingered on Gillian's face vanished as she warmed to her subject. Monopolising the conversation, she went into great lengths explaining to Mandy how she had fought this battle and that with the various builders, plumbers, decorators, to achieve her plans for the house. She continued throughout dinner — a meal she seemed to take quite for granted but which was a banquet for

20

Mandy, living as she did on Mrs Phillips' plain uninspired suppers and a sandwich for lunch at the office. The portions of duck following on the smoked salmon were too much for her unaccustomed stomach to cope with and despite Jon's exhortations to try something off the sweet trolley, she was unable to do so.

'I don't think you've been eating enough, Mandy!' he said as he ordered coffee. 'You've lost a great deal of weight since I last saw you.'

'Don't be silly, Jon. No girl wants to be fat these days. I can tell you, Mandy, I have quite a job to keep my weight down. As a matter of fact, I've just found a new diet. It's really fabulous.'

The conversation turned once more on herself, Gillian rambled on whilst they drank their coffee and returned to the lounge. Jon seemed to have given up trying to participate. He sat smoking one cigarette after another, his eyes for the most part on his wife's face, only occasionally turning to Mandy with a smile she described to herself as sympathetic.

He's not happy! she thought, losing the thread of Gillian's conversation. There were moments when his expression was almost bitter. Yet she was sure he loved his wife. Something in his eyes when they rested on Gillian's beautiful face made her certain he was still enthralled by her.

'How long a holiday do you have?' she asked him as Gillian paused to light a cigarette.

'Our week's up tomorrow!' he told her. 'The locum I managed to get leaves at teatime so we've got to be back by then. It's gone terribly quickly.'

'A week is perfectly ridiculous!' Gillian said. 'I told Jon it was hardly worth having a holiday if we couldn't have two weeks at least. God knows he works hard enough. We've really only had five days, seeing that Jon was determined to make a stop to see you on the way home.'

Mandy felt the colour rising in her cheeks.

'I didn't realise you came to Clinton on purpose,' she said awkwardly. 'I thought you were driving through here anyway. It was . . . very kind of you!'

Jon looked embarrassed. He'd told Mandy on the phone that they were dropping in on their way back.

'It's barely out of our way,' he said awkwardly.

'It was very kind of you anyway,' Mandy put in quickly. 'I've had a marvellous meal and the whole evening has been a great treat for me.' She glanced at her watch and stood up. 'I'll really have to go,' she added. 'I told my baby-minder I wouldn't be late.'

Neither Jon nor Gillian made any effort to detain her. There was a short discussion as to where they would meet with Timmy in the morning.

'He might be a bit of nuisance in the hotel,' Mandy said, sensing that Gillian would not be any too pleased to have the child crawling round the lounge. 'As it is Saturday, Mrs Phillips will be out shopping, so I'm sure she wouldn't mind a bit if I asked you round to my digs.'

It was agreed that Jon and Gillian would arrive soon after ten next day and Jon escorted Mandy into the lobby.

'Have you far to go?' he asked solicitously. 'Could I run you back in the car?'

'It's really not too far and I like walking!' Mandy refused the offer. She was painfully aware of Gillian, bored and resentful of this interruption to her holiday, waiting for Jon in the lounge. 'Thanks again and good night.'

He seemed about to say something, but in the end remained standing silently watching her as she went out of the door. As she turned once to wave, she thought his face looked indescribably tired and somehow filled with sadness. His expression haunted her inexplicably as she walked quickly home.

2

He lay in bed watching Gillian as she sat at the dressing table removing her make-up. This usually took a full quarter of an hour and the operation was always carried out in her scanty underwear.

When they were first married he had found this intensely exciting. Her beautiful body was almost totally exposed, he would lie in anticipation of the love-making that would follow, watching the lift of her breasts as she raised her hands to her forehead or long dark hair; waiting for the moment when she would peel off her tights and run her beautiful hands the full length of her smooth white legs. His physical need of her was continuous and intense and not always requited. There had been many nights when, after this tantalising unconscious display, she would fall into bed saying:

'God, I'm tired!' or 'I've a splitting headache!' She even said occasionally: 'I don't feel like it tonight, Jon!' as he reached out his arms to hold her. Pride forbade any argument on the subject and a respect for her feelings which she didn't seem to reciprocate. Gradually over the months, and now years, he had ceased to give any indications of his own need but waited for her to make the initial demands. These had become less and less frequent as their bedtime conversation became the hour for him to listen to Gillian's complaints. Sometimes, not often, he would shut off his ears so that her voice was only a faint murmur in his mind whilst he tried to think of nothing but how beautiful she was, how desirable, how much he wanted to make love to her. Occasionally she sensed his intention and was furiously angry with him.

'You're always too busy to listen during the day and when I do get a chance for a word with my own husband you're thinking of sex. You're revolting!'

Hurt, humiliated and with a growing sense of inadequacy, he would turn away from her beauty and when Gillian finally came to bed they would sleep back to back without touching.

She talked now as he watched her.

'Deadly boring evening, Jon. I don't see why you should have to make yourself responsible for Peter's little bastard. It's the girl's own fault she's in this mess and it's no concern of ours.'

'Gillian, we've been through this before. Illegitimate or not, the child is my nephew, Pete's child. I don't expect you to care but I do.'

She flashed him a quick satisfied look.

'You said it, Jon, not me. It's your concern, not mine. So that lets me out, doesn't it? I told you I didn't want to go and coo over the baby tomorrow and you were the one who said I'd have to. Well, I'm not going. You can go if you want, but I'm not interested. I'm sorry for Mandy, but that's as far as it goes.'

'She says the child is lovely!' Jon spoke without thinking. His voice held a note of wistfulness that did not escape her. She glanced at him sharply.

'I hope you're not going to start all that again, Jon. I don't think I could stand it tonight!'

He knew without asking what 'all that' referred to — his desperate pleas for her to have a child. He used every argument he could think of, not least her continual cry of boredom. With a child to look after the days wouldn't seem so long or tedious or empty. Her reply was always the same.

'If you think I'm going to be tied any more than I am already being a doctor's wife, you're mistaken. I don't want a baby.'

Only once had he been stung to remind her that marriage was a partnership and *he* wanted children.

'You knew that before you married me,' he remonstrated. 'You can't go back on it now, Gilly.'

'Okay, so I'll have children one day. But not yet, Jon. I'm only twenty-four. Besides, we can't afford it. If we can't afford a decent car how do you think we can cope with all the expenses a child would mean? Be realistic, darling. Let's get ourselves organised first. Just be patient, sweetie.'

He'd been patient a long time and he was beginning to realize that the wait might be a good deal longer still. There was always something Gilly wanted — new curtains, a holiday in Majorca, a new outfit. They never saved money. Gilly spent it as fast as he acquired it and ran through her own allowance, too. She had a little over a thousand a year from her father as pocket money — a gift Jon secretly resented but did not feel justified in objecting to since he had little enough to give Gilly. She'd grown up used to money and he knew it wasn't easy for her living on a young doctor's income. Both Gilly and her father had always expected she would marry money and he, Jon, was still surprised and humble that she had finally agreed to marry him. Sometimes he wondered why she had done so. He suspected that sex was the major factor. Physically they were totally compatible, their love-making wild and unrestrained and passionate. Gillian, before marriage, had been insatiable and neither was content to be apart for long.

But that changed. Their mutual need for one another had become his need, suppressed, muted, no longer the spontaneous outpourings of passion it had once been. He felt all too often now as if he were only a participant required to satisfy Gilly's needs. It was each time a little less tender, wilder and quickly over. Gilly read avidly any new book on sex on the market. She was always trying out new techniques as if it were essential for her to extract the maximum sensation out of the act of love rather than desirous of sharing love with him. It wasn't what he wanted but he still needed her and wanted her badly enough to accept her terms.

'You aren't listening to a word I'm saying, Jon!' Gilly's voice filled with irritation broke in on his thoughts. 'I meant what I said, you know. I'm not going with you tomorrow.'

'Okay, I heard!' He wasn't going to start an argument now, although he felt bitterly that she might make the effort for his sake if not for Mandy's. That poor girl had suffered enough indignities without Gilly making it obvious that she disapproved. On the other hand, her absence might be preferable to her indifference, if not dislike, of the small boy around whom Mandy's life revolved. He could think up some excuse for Gilly not being with him — illness, perhaps.

'Well, at least you understand my point of view for once,' Gillian was saying as she removed the last traces of cleansing cream and began to brush her hair. 'I suppose the evening wasn't too bad really.' Her voice softened a tone. 'It was a damn good dinner, better than I expected. It's not a bad hotel. What's the bed like — comfortable?'

She gave him a quick meaningful smile.

'Warm up my side for me!' she said, her voice now soft and languorous, her eyes half closed as she stared at him across the room.

He felt his pulses stirring. Gillian's change of mood meant only one thing and he knew that this would be one of the nights when she wanted him to make love to her. Earlier, when they had been changing for dinner, he'd wanted her so desperately that he had hurried his own dressing and left the room before he found himself pleading with her when she was clearly not in the mood. Even his kiss had irritated her. Now, suddenly, he was tired — tired of thinking, of worrying, of trying to fathom out this strange young wife of his. He wanted her but not the way it would be tonight. He would have liked her soft and warm and loving, the passion between them rising slowly and tenderly. He would like to make gentle love.

'Hey, Sleepyhead. Open your eyes!'

She had taken off her underclothes and was wearing a thin transparent blue négligé. She came across the room smiling, her face devoid of make-up but still beautiful. Her eyes were brilliant and taunting. She lay down beside him, her face so close she was almost touching.

'Kiss?' she said, her mouth wet and provocative.

As he lifted his mouth to hers, she bit him suddenly on the lower lip so that he winced.

'Awake now?' she whispered.

'Yes, I'm awake!' he answered, as with a long sigh he drew her warm shuddering body against him, knowing that his resistance was only in his mind and could not last for long.

★　★　★

His first sight of Mandy's child was strangely unnerving. Timmy reminded

33

him instantly and painfully of his dead brother. The resemblance was so marked, he thought bitterly, that were Gilly here she'd never again make one of her occasional snide remarks that Mandy's child could be any man's for all Jon knew.

The little boy stared back at him — a solemn unblinking stare that made him laugh.

'Doesn't he know it's rude to stare like that!' he said. Mandy smiled back.

'Unfortunately, good manners are not yet a part of his curriculum. Stop it, Timmy!'

'Obedience isn't part of his curriculum either,' Jon laughed again, as the little boy toddled closer for a better look at the stranger towering above him. Jon knelt down so that his face was on a level with the child's.

'There!' he said. 'Now you can really see me!'

Encouraged by the laughter in the man's eyes, Timmy's face crinkled slowly into a smile. Jon caught his breath.

'He could be Pete!' he murmured.

Mandy nodded.

'I know. Their smiles are identical. I'm lucky, aren't I?'

He looked at her curiously.

'I suppose you are. I never thought of it quite like that, but having Timmy must be like having a little bit of Pete still around. You loved my brother very much, didn't you?'

'Yes. At least, I think I did. I know this may sound awful, but it all seems such a long while ago now. I only knew him such a short while. It almost seems like a dream now, perhaps because so much has happened since.'

The little boy, now completely at ease, was holding out his arms to be lifted up. Jon did so and sat down on a chair with the boy on his knee where he became instantly absorbed in Jon's watch.

Mandy smiled.

'You look as if you've been coping

35

with babies all your life,' she said. 'But then I suppose you have quite a bit of experience with them as a doctor. I hadn't a clue when I had Timmy. I've had to go by instinct.'

'Then your instinct has been infallible!' Jon said approvingly. 'He's a beautiful healthy little boy. I congratulate you. It can't have been easy, Mandy?'

'Not always. I think there have been moments when I've felt desperately alone and I'd have given my right arm to be able to go home to my parents.'

'They aren't reconciled, then?'

Mandy shook her head.

'You can't really expect them to be. Dad's a county councillor and terribly conventional. I think even if he wanted to forgive me he couldn't bring himself to face what the neighbours would say. Mother writes to me sometimes. I think she'd like to see her grandchild, but she won't go against Dad. I get depressed sometimes thinking what they miss — and Timmy. Dad would be good for him. He loves men and I get quite embarrassed sometimes when I take him to the park. He'll smile at some strange male and hold out his arms to be lifted up. Sometimes, if it's someone who's embarrassed or irritated by this unasked for display of affection, I feel like going up and saying: 'Don't be cross with him. He hasn't got a father of his own. Couldn't you be a father just for a few minutes!' Dad could have been a compensation if he'd wanted.'

Jon, watching the girl's mobile, sensitive, hurt little face, felt a pang of protectiveness. The girl his brother had chosen had courage and more even than he'd realised. She wasn't the tough self-sufficient type he'd half supposed her to be. Seeing her now, in jeans and a skinny rib jersey, he noticed how painfully thin she was and wondered if she got enough to eat.

'Your landlady?' he asked. 'Does she look after you properly? Feed you well?'

'Oh, she has a heart of gold beneath that Victorian exterior. She's always buying little titbits for Timmy, and once, last winter when I was ill, she looked after him for two whole days when I couldn't get him to the day nursery. She's very kind.'

'And you manage okay for money? If Pete had lived . . . '

'Yes, I know. But I earn enough to keep us both. I'm all right. We both are!'

She's proud! Jon told himself. I mustn't abuse that pride! At the same time he wanted passionately to do something for her. He looked down at the boy and felt a sudden rush of emotion. He was his own flesh and blood — even, since he looked so like Pete, looked like him, too. It could be his child. But not his and Gilly's. The little boy had Mandy's nose and chin, small, square, determined.

'I envy you!' he said simply. 'He's a wonderful kid!'

Aware of the wistfulness in his tone, Mandy said quickly:

'But you'll soon be having children of

your own. You're fond of them, aren't you?'

Jon frowned.

'Yes, of course, but we can't really afford . . . ' He broke off, conscious of the stupidity of the remark. He didn't believe it himself — it was Gilly's argument. If Mandy could support herself and Timmy on her meagre income . . .

'I expect we'll get around to it soon,' he said with an attempted smile. 'Gilly's been pretty busy doing the house and getting used to being a doctor's wife.'

Mandy was far too kind to remind him that most of his wife's remarks the previous evening hd been punctuated with the fact that she was frantically bored.

The silence between them became prolonged and awkward. Mandy said brightly:

'Well, you'll have to borrow Timmy sometimes. I could certainly do with a break, especially when he's cutting a tooth. He's a positive horror then. I don't get any sleep and then I drop off at work next day. He's due another tooth soon. I'll post him off to you the moment he starts yelling.'

As if he understood his mother's words, Timmy suddenly climbed down from Jon's knee and ran across the room to his mother. She laughed and pulled him into her arms.

'Well, maybe I won't send you away. You don't mean to be difficult, do you, darling?'

Jon felt his heart give a strange little twist. The tenderness in Mandy's voice was oddly touching. He saw her with new eyes, as a woman rather than a girl, and found himself wondering if she had been this way with Pete. Some women were born maternal; knew the need men had for being comforted and encouraged and consoled. Lucky Pete! he thought. At least he knew real love for a little while before he died. Had he appreciated it? Or had he taken Mandy for granted in that casual carefree way he accepted everything that happened to him? He found himself hoping very much that Pete had made her happy.

'You must get a holiday sometime,' he said impulsively. 'Why don't you come and stay with us? We've a nice garden Timmy could play in and the house is plenty big enough to accommodate you without anyone noticing. Do come, Mandy. I'd love the chance to get to know Timmy better and . . . '

He'd been about to say 'Gilly would love it, too!' but he knew before the words were out that here was one good reason Mandy could not come. Gilly would hate it.

The same thought had crossed Mandy's mind. She knew exactly what caused that look of embarrassment on Jon's face and said quickly:

'I'd love to come sometime but I won't be due a holiday until next summer. Maybe then. We'll see!'

They both understood each other very well. Their eyes met, smiled briefly and turned away to look at the child rather than at each other's discomfort.

Mandy felt desperately sorry for him. He was turning out to be very different from Pete, who just laughed his way through life. Jon cared deeply, felt things deeply, and, by the look of it, his marriage was not terribly happy. He and Gilly did not seem well suited to one another, yet she could understand how they'd fallen in love. Gillian was beautiful with her fabulous face and body. And Jon was very attractive. She could well imagine herself falling in love with someone like Jon, kind, dependable, sensitive and yet essentially masculine in his good looks.

'I'd give a lot to know what you were thinking, Mandy. Mona Lisa has nothing on your smile. A penny for them.'

She felt herself flushing a deep red. It was as if he had caught her out in some indiscretion.

'They aren't worth it!' she said, attempting a smile.

Jon tried to subdue his curiosity, the greater since that shy smile of hers. He felt as if he had somehow embarrassed her. Her face and the ever-changing expression in her eyes interested him. Without being beautiful, she was oddly attractive, one minute innocent girl and the next mature woman. He tried to remember her exact age — nineteen, twenty? She seemed years and years younger than Gilly, yet she was the mother of a year-old child.

'Do you ever regret . . . anything?' he asked hesitantly.

Mandy's smile was reassuring.

'How could I when I have Timmy? Maybe it hasn't been easy, but he's worth all the loneliness and struggle. If I knew what would happen and had my life to lead over again, I'd do the same. I couldn't think of a life without him now.'

'Will you promise me that if ever you get into difficulties — financial or othewise — you'll get in touch with me? Things could happen which might make it difficult for you to keep him. Promise me you'll let me help if . . . '

'Yes, of course,' she said simply. She gave him a quick smile. 'I know I'm proud but I'd swallow my pride any day rather than lose Timmy.'

He smiled back at her.

'I'm glad to hear it. Will you write to me occasionally? Send snaps if you have any? Now we've really met and I've seen my little nephew, I don't want to lose touch.'

'Yes, of course. It'll be nice for me to know someone somewhere is interested in us. When Timmy cut a tooth or when he took his first step I'd no one to tell — except Mrs Phillips and the girls at work. I suppose it sounds silly but I felt really miserable at such times. I'd have given a lot to be able to rush to the nearest telephone and ring Mother, to tell her the news.

'Then the next time, the next tooth, ring me! Here's my number — it's the surgery number, actually. My secretary always knows where I am. If I'm not in leave a number where I can phone you back. Okay?'

Once again Gillian's name was not mentioned. Mandy wondered whether Jon had suggested the surgery number other than his house number because of Gillian. Not that she, Mandy, had any cause to feel guilty about the deception, if there were one. It was not as if she were about to embark on a secret affair with Jon! The thought made her smile to herself and again Jon noticed the little lift of her mouth and found himself longing to know what thought was bringing that strange quirk to her lips.

For a few minutes longer he played with the boy on the floor, heedless of his good slacks and shirt. Mandy made coffee which they drank whilst Timmy had his mid-morning milk. Then Jon said he would have to go.

'I really don't want to in the least!' he told her reluctantly. 'But Gilly wants to leave before lunch. We've some friends of hers coming in for drinks this evening and she wants to get home to prepare for them.'

It was only after he had left, in the curiously deflated atmosphere his departure evoked, that Mandy thought of that last remark and what it revealed. He had spoken of Gilly's friends, not his, not 'ours'. No wonder he had been reluctant to go.

She stooped and took the little boy into her arms, hugging him closely.

'Poor Jon!' she said to the indifferent child. 'Poor Jon is lonely — even lonelier than I am, since I, at least, have you!'

*　*　*

As the car sped smoothly down the motorway eating up the miles as it took them nearer and nearer home, Gillian said sharply:

'For heaven's sake stop moping about that girl, Jon. I'm beginning to wish you'd never gone to see her. For the ninetieth time, she's not *your* worry. If she's lonely, it's her own fault. She could have had the child adopted and I told her so that day at the home. She wouldn't listen, so now she has no one but herself to blame if she's saddled with him and can't get out.'

'I don't think Mandy sees it like that. She told me she'd make the same decision all over again if she had another chance.'

Gillian grimaced.

'Then she must be out of her mind! Honestly, Jon, I hope you didn't encourage her. Girls like that get away with it once and then go and do it again if you give them half a chance.'

'Stop it, Gillian!' Jon's voice was sharp enough to put a temporary end to his wife's moralising. 'You don't know what you are talking about. Mandy loves the boy and she's not really lonely at all whilst she has him. You wouldn't be so lonely either if you had a charming little boy like Timmy to care for.'

'Oh, God, so that's it. Can't you drop it just for once, Jon? I must have been out of my mind, letting you within miles of that kid. Now I supose I'll have nothing but 'Why can't we have a baby?' till I'm crazy. Well, let's get this quite straight once and for all. The answer is no, no, *no!* Not yet, maybe not ever, if you keep nagging me about it. You've no right to ask me, anyway. It isn't you who has to carry it around for nine bloody months, give birth to it and then wash its dirty nappies. I'd have to, not you, so it's my job, not yours, to say if and when I want a kid. As of this minute, I don't.'

Jon's face was dark with anger.

'It may interest you to know that as of this minute I don't either. Any woman who thinks and feels like you ought to be sterilised at birth. You aren't fit to have a child. You're the most selfish woman I know.'

For a moment Gillian was too surprised to speak. A long childhood spent with an adoring father who spoilt her and indulged her had immunised her against criticism. From the expensive girls' boarding school he sent her to, where she disliked and was disliked by the other pupils, he had removed her at once. From then on she had lived at home, petted, adored and admired by everyone around her. Her natural beauty as she developed from girl to woman ensured the uncritical admiration of every young male who came within her orbit.

Partly from boredom, partly from vanity, she became a model and was, with her casual self-assurance and sophisticated gracefulness, an instant success. Having all the money she needed from her father, she worked only when she pleased and then chiefly because she liked to see herself on magazine covers or advertising posters. Nobody criticised her, least of all Jon, whom she had met quite by chance and who had fallen in love with her on sight.

At first it had amused her to flirt with the quiet handsome young medical student — one of the many admirers who haunted the house. But he soon came to stand out from the others. His refusal to put a date with her before his work became a challenge. The more adamantly he refused to cut his lectures or give up an evening earmarked for study, the more urgent became her desire to dominate him. She found herself thinking about him all the time. He was totally different from the wealthy young set normally enjoying her father's hospitality and from which she knew her father would be happy to see her choose a husband.

Despite Jon's attraction for her, the idea of marrying him did not really occur to her as anything but ridiculous, in fact it might never have come to marriage had her father not flatly refused even to consider the penniless student as a possible son-in-law. For the first time in her life her father said 'No.' Immediately Gillian decided to prove she could get her own way. She succeeded only in part. Her father's threat to cut her off without the proverbial penny, pushed her into a register office and a hurried wedding as means to defy him. She was confident her father would relent after the deed was done. To her dismay, he did so only to the tune of a miserly allowance of a few hundred a year.

'And not a penny more, Gilly. It'll be interesting to see how long you last as a poor man's wife. Not long, I imagine. Anyway, the experience will be good for you. You're spoilt!'

Gillian was furious but not really daunted by the prospect of marriage with Jon. Money did not seem too important at first. She believed she was really in love and Jon worshipped her. Living together under the same roof certainly made their love-life a lot easier, too. When Jon was not working they were in bed — or so it seemed, their passion urgent and mutual and intensely satisfying. She basked in Jon's adoration, believing that now he was her husband he would behave as her father had, indulging every whim. But he had remained steadfastly immovable

with regard to his work. It came first
— always. Not even the sexual hold she
had over him would keep him in bed
with her if a patient needed him.

For a year she tried to compete
against her only rival. Then she gave up.
Trying to seduce Jon into putting her
first had been a novelty she soon tired
of. She derived less and less satisfaction
from this side of her marriage and none
at all from the rest of it. She was not cut
out to be a doctor's wife and she was
bored by her neighbours. With time to
consider what a mess she had made of
her life, she grew daily less willing to be
the kind of wife Jon wanted. But no
matter how badly she behaved, Jon
never complained, never criticised her,
never showed his impatience or irritation or disappointment. Until this
moment in the car he had never spoken
unkindly or harshly to her and therefore
she took note of it. *You're the most
selfish woman I know.*

Maybe it was true, she thought. And
if it was, did she care? Wasn't Jon

equally selfish, putting his career before her as if she, his wife, were only of secondary importance to him.

Her silence, so unusual and unexpected, affected Jon in a way her sarcasm would not have done. In a conciliatory tone of voice he said:

'Look, Gilly, I may have spoken a bit unkindly. I'm sorry. We seem to have been on the edge of a quarrel for ages and in a way I'm glad it has come to a head. I'll admit I'm more than a bit upset that you don't want a child. When people fall in love and get married, having children seems . . . I don't know . . . a natural follow-up. I've waited nearly two years for you to agree. Seeing that little boy — well, it crystallised my suppressed longing to have one of my own — your child, Gilly. I suppose I was a bit hurt because you don't feel the same way, so I tried to hurt you. I'm sorry, darling.'

She was mollified by his apology, her self-assurance restored. For one moment she thought he'd fallen out of love with her! She fell back on her usual excuse.

'I may seem the selfish one to you, Jon, but aren't you being a bit selfish, too, wanting to tie me down to the nursery when I've barely left it myself? I am only twenty-four. We've years and years ahead to have kids. Why now? I'm young and I want to have a good time. Is that so wrong?' She sensed that these arguments were not softening him and added persuasively: 'I know you want children, darling, but I want you all to myself for a bit longer. I see little enough of you as it is without having to share your time and love with anyone else.'

He reached out at once and gave her knee a squeeze.

'I do understand, darling. In a way I feel the same. We don't get much time to do all the things we want. That's the trouble with being a doctor — you belong first of all to your patients. But believe me, Gilly, if I could be with you more often . . .'

He broke off abruptly, realising that he was treading on dangerous ground. Gillian wanted to write to her father and ask for a bigger allowance so that he could afford to take on a partner. At the moment, large though it was and growing daily, the practice did not warrant and could not afford two doctors. He and Gillian had argued about it endlessly, Jon trying to point out that to accept help from her father undermined him, struck at his masculine pride; Gillian telling him he was selfish and old-fashioned, that her father's money would be as impersonal as a bank lending cash for a business enterprise.

But Jon knew it would be different. Though Gillian argued that he could pay back her father when he could afford to, she did not seem to realise that he would be unlikely to have any cash to spare for years to come. They could barely manage with only themselves to support and with the advent of children . . .

'Perhaps you are right about waiting a while yet for a family,' he said thoughtfully. 'Maybe I should get the practice better established first and that could mean a year or more.'

Gillian relaxed, smiling and happy now that she thought she had won the day. She was fully prepared to be pleasant to Jon for the rest of the journey home. She felt as if they had crossed a rather difficult hurdle in their marriage and that Jon at last was beginning to see for himself that a child was the very last thing he or she needed. They drove home without raising the subject again.

3

The rest of the month slipped by almost unnoticed by Jon. But for the fact that Gillian was immersed in preparations for Christmas he would not have been aware that the festivities were close at hand. As it was, seldom a day went past without her informing him that she was accepting this invitation or that to parties hc was far from sure he'd be able to attend. Gillian seemed happy and excited with so much entertainment to look forward to. He did not have the heart to act as a wet blanket by telling her that he really had no inclination to go on an endless round of cocktail and dinner parties, especially if he were called out the previous night and was, as so often happened, desperately short of sleep.

With some dismay he watched the total of seasonal 'flu cases mount slowly but certainly towards a minor epidemic. Only then did he warn Gillian that he might have to spend his Christmas working.

'But you can't, Jon. I've committed us to . . . '

'Darling, I'm just letting you know that it *could* happen, not that I'm calling off anything as yet,' he explained patiently. 'People understand last-minute cancellations from a doctor. Anyway, there's nothing to stop you going even if I'm unable to do so.'

On the point of a row, Gillian decided at the last minute to hold her castigations until the worst actually happened. Since Jon had stopped nagging her about having a baby, they'd been getting along much better. She'd recently made friends with a girl called Patty Sinclair, much the same age as herself, with two very attractive bachelor brothers. School friends of Patty's husband, Jock, the four of them lived in a huge Victorian house on the edge of town, having what seemed to Gillian to be one long party.

The two brothers, Geoff and Mike, had bought the largest of the local estate agencies and Patty worked as secretary-receptionist for them. Not that any of them ever seemed to do much work, for they were always roaring around the countryside in Geoff's Volvo, ostensibly viewing properties but taking in lunch or a pub crawl on the way. Gillian sometimes went with them and felt as if she was back in the days preceding her marriage when life was carefree and hectic and fun and responsibilities weren't the overriding reason for not doing what one wanted.

Both young men were attracted by her and Gillian enjoyed flirting with them, playing one against the other but without getting too deeply involved with either. It was harmless and amusing and the boredom of her home life was a thing of the past. Jon seemed delighted that she had found a way to pass the time and only once raised an objection following the first occasion she had invited all the Sinclair ménage to dinner. Polite and hospitable as always, it was not until they were gone that Jon said:

'I don't know that I would altogether trust that lot, Gilly. They're a bit crazy, if you ask me.'

'That's what makes them fun!' she had flashed back. 'I don't see why everyone has to be cast in the same mould as you, Jon. *They* aren't bowed down beneath the weight of sick patients!'

He'd looked upset at the jibe, but had maintained control of himself.

'I know it's a bore being married to a doctor, Gilly, but you are my wife for better or for worse and, as such, you can't afford to be too crazy or it will reflect on me. You do understand, darling?'

Afraid that he would start nagging her to stop seeing so much of Patty and her family, Gillian appeared to see Jon's point of view and promised to go carefully. Now, with Christmas almost upon them and Jon telling her he might have to work if the 'flu epidemic got worse, it crossed Gillian's mind that it really would not matter so much if he were tied up. Either Geoff or Mike would be only too happy to act as her escort. There was the New Year's Eve dinner and dance at the big roadhouse she'd persuaded Jon to book. If he couldn't go, she'd get one of the boys to take her.

The epidemic grew and Jon's secretary, the middle-aged Miss Hill, succumbed. Jon was forced to ask Gillian to take telephone calls in his absence. It was obvious to her that *someone* had to do so when he was out on his calls, but after two days of coping with anxious wives and mothers who forever seemed to be telephoning for Jon's help or advice, together with coping at the ghastly morning and evening surgery, Gillian knew that she had had enough.

'It's simply not my scene, Jon. I hate it and I hate sick people. You've *got* to get a replacement for Miss Hill.'

White with exhaustion, Jon stared at his wife uncomprehendingly.

'But you know I tried the agency. It's the same everywhere, Gilly. Everyone is short-staffed with people down with 'flu.'

'Then get on to a London agency. There must be someone!'

But there was no one to step into Miss Hill's shoes. Jon's hopes that she would be back at work at the end of the week were soon dashed. The 'flu developed into bronchitis and mild pneumonia and he himself took her into hospital.

He dreaded his return home and having to tell Gillian that she must cope for at least three weeks longer. He hated to ask her, but he simply had no alternative.

Gillian, however, had found one. As Jon, a stiff whisky in one hand and a cigarette in the other, haltingly tried to break the news, Gillian went to the mantelpiece and took down a letter.

'Read it!' she said curtly.

Although addressed to both of them, Jon knew it had been written really to him. His own worries forgotten, he digested Mandy's news.

I'm afraid things are rather tough at the moment as our new boss has decided to close down the Personal Service side of the business. In future it's all to be done by computers and though I do understand the need for economy, it in effect puts me out of a job. Married women, and I count as that because of Timmy, are first to go and after Christmas four of the most recently employed girls will have to leave, too.

I've been trying to get another job but everyone seems to want a secretary who will work alternate Saturdays and I think I told you, the day nursery doesn't open at the weekends so I can't fill the vacancies I might otherwise have fitted.

I'm afraid this letter sounds rather like one long moan but I'm not so much complaining as feeling desperate. Mrs Phillips has been incredibly kind and told me to forget the rent until I'm back at work. She even offered to look after Timmy for me on Saturdays but although she copes with baby-sitting at night, she's really not able to manage him in the daytime.

I'm writing really in the very faint hope that you might know of someone in need of a nine-to-five secretary, no Saturdays, and if you would be good enough to recommend me. I do have excellent shorthand and typing speeds. Although I hate the thought of leaving Mrs Phillips as she has been so kind and really loves Timmy, I need work more than kindness! I think when you were last here you told me there was a very good nursery for babies of working mothers, so you seemed the obvious person to write to in Pewly.

If you can help, I'd be so grateful,
Yours,
Mandy

'Poor kid!' Jon said. 'What rotten luck! Perhaps . . . '

'For her maybe, but not for us,' Gillian broke in. 'Don't you see, Jon, *you* can use her — anyway, for the time Miss Hill is away. If she's useless, you can always push her off elsewhere when Miss Hill gets back. At least it would be someone to answer the phone and deal with that ghastly horde of people queuing in the surgery. She wants work and you need a worker. What could be more opportune?'

Jon allowed her suggestion to seep through the weariness that was rapidly overtaking him in the warmth of the room and with the relaxing aid of the whisky. Gillian's idea made good sense. Mandy needed a job and he desperately needed a helper. But was it fair to uproot her from her landlady if he didn't intend to give her a permanent job? And where would she live? The day nursery for Timmy would be no problem. As visiting doctor he could fix that.

'Well, what's making you hesitate?' Gillian asked. 'Why not ring Mandy before she goes and finds a job elsewhere? We don't want someone else to snap her up.'

'She couldn't come here at a moment's notice . . . '

'Oh, don't *make* difficulties, Jon. Here is the answer to all our problems and it'll answer hers, too. If I have to, I'll drive down and collect her myself, help her pack up or whatever you think she needs to have done to get her here.'

'But she hasn't anywhere to live, Gilly. We'd have to find accommodation for her first.'

'Give her and the kid the spare room, if that's all that's stopping you. *I* don't care just so long as I don't have to lift that damn telephone once more and say 'Yes, Mrs Smith, and what's his temperature, Mrs Smith, and has little George been sick, Mrs Smith?' It's not on, Jon. I can't and I won't.'

He nodded. It wasn't Gillian's fault she was failing to be a good doctor's assistant. He'd married her expecting her to be his wife, not his unpaid help. Not that he had realised she had this built-in antipathy to sick people — but then she couldn't help that either. He had a built-in antipathy to cats he couldn't overcome.

With hindsight, he should have joined the group practice where a number of doctors shared the work and an adequate staff. But he'd wanted to run his practice in his own way. He'd reconsider it at a more suitable moment but meanwhile, his thoughts swung back to Mandy. He could be doing her a kindness. Christmas in lodgings with a child and no money wouldn't be much fun for her. At least if she came here he'd see the boy had plenty of new toys and he and Mandy would get the right nourishing food they needed. She was far too thin. If Gillian was willing to have her living with them there would be no rent problem.

'I've got two more calls to make before dinner,' he said. 'Could you find out Mandy's telephone number and ring her for me? I simply haven't time. Ask her if she'd like to come and, if she would, make any arrangements you think fit.'

Gillian let out her breath. She had been very much afraid Jon was on the point of refusing. Now, left to her own devices, she had no doubt that she could persuade Mandy to come. When she wanted something badly enough she usually got it.

As Jon went out of the front door, she lifted the telephone and dialled directory enquiries. Five minutes later she was speaking to Mandy.

'It's Jon's wife, Gillian!' she said. 'Jon and I got your letter today and we've both been worried to death about you.'

'But there's no need for that!' Mandy said, sounding embarrassed. 'I wouldn't have written except that . . . '

'You need work. I quite understand,' Gillian broke in smoothly. 'And you can't know how opportune your letter is, Mandy. Poor Jon is up to his eyes with the 'flu epidemic and his secretary-receptionist has been packed off to hospital with pneumonia. He's desperate for help, Mandy, and on the mat drops your letter saying you are desperate for work. Isn't it a wonderful coincidence?'

It was a few minutes before Mandy understood what Gillian was suggesting.

'Are you absolutely *sure* you want me?' she asked hesitatingly. 'This isn't Jon's way — your way of being charitable?'

Gillian laughed.

'Far from it! We'll both welcome you with open arms, my dear, and that's the truth!'

Mandy heard the ring of conviction and took a deep breath.

'Obviously I'm free to come and help as best I can,' she said, 'although I've no medical experience. And are you quite sure you want Timmy in the house? He'd be at the nursery all day but there'd be evenings and weekends; though naturally I'd keep him out of yours and Jon's way.'

'My dear girl, we'd be delighted to have the boy here. You know how fond of children Jon is and I'm already planning a Christmas tree and a stocking for Timmy.'

Mandy felt suddenly guilty. She had entirely misjudged Gillian, thinking her hard and unfeeling and here she was being charming and warm-hearted, thinking of Timmy when she might have been complaining at having strangers in her home at Christmas.

'It is good of you, Gillian,' she said. 'I'm so very grateful. It all seems too good to be true.'

'That's settled then,' Gillian said, cutting short Mandy's thanks. 'Now how soon could you get here, Mandy? If I were to drive down tomorrow after lunch, could you be packed up and ready to leave?'

'Tomorrow? I suppose I could!' Mandy agreed. 'It would be easier certainly if you are picking me up in the car — I don't have to sort things out for packing if I can just lump Timmy's toys and buggy and things into the boot. Are you sure, Gillian? It's an awful bore for you.'

'But I'll be delighted!' Gillian said. 'And so will Jon when I tell him the good news. So that's agreed. I'll fetch you tomorrow, Mandy, about two-thirty, okay?'

Mandy replaced the receiver and when she had recovered her breath and her equilibrium she went to tell Mrs Phillips the astonishing results of her phone call.

'It's almost too good to be true, isn't it?' she said happily. 'Though I shall hate saying goodbye to you, Mrs Phillips. You've been wonderful to me and to Timmy. We'll never forget you or your kindness!'

To her consternation she saw tears in her landlady's eyes.

'I never thought as how I could grow so fond of a girl who'd done the wrong you did, Mandy, still less love the offspring of such immorality.' Mrs

Phillips sniffed and blew her nose. 'Not that I'm condoning what you did, my girl. I'll never do that. But I find myself respecting you all the same. You've got courage and you've been the best mother you knew how. As for Timmy . . . I'll confess he's a dear little boy with only good in him. I'll not forget either of you and I'll miss you both, Timmy especially.'

Mandy felt a lump in her throat. It was hard to believe Mrs Phillips could relax so far as to admit she cared about them.

'I'll write to you!' she promised, knowing Mrs Phillips would never stoop to asking her to do so. 'And I'll send photos of Timmy. Perhaps we could come and visit you sometimes.'

There was an angry snort.

'If you came near this town and didn't stop by to see me it would be the last time I'd speak to you!' she said paradoxically. 'Now off with you and start that packing. I'll put Timmy to bed for you.'

Mandy began her packing with nervous excitement. She found it difficult to believe that this time tomorrow night she and Timmy would be in a new room in Jon's house, on the brink of a new job. Everything had happened so totally unexpectedly and so fast! She would be sad to leave the only home and friend she and Timmy had, but at the same time it would be wonderful to be in a real home again. Gillian had sounded warm and friendly. Maybe they would become good friends. Her life had been starved of companionship and Timmy was too young to compensate for the company of other young people of her own age. It would be wonderful working for Jon whom she felt she already knew and liked. She hoped she would be adequate help for him. Although she had confidence in her ability to be a first-class secretary, able to cope without supervision and to tackle problems intelligently and responsibly, she was still not certain if she could be of much help to him on the medical side. It might be some time before she became used to the various forms and medical terms and even to learn the names of all his patients. No doubt Gillian would be there to help her, she consoled herself.

As she hurriedly emptied drawers and folded her clothes, a little of Mandy's self-confidence evaporated. It seemed almost too coincidental that Jon should need her the very day her letter arrived asking him to find a job for her. On reflection, it began to appear unlikely. Even if his secretary was away, he had Gillian. Although on that one encounter with Jon's wife Mandy would not have thought Gillian exactly fitted to be a secretary-receptionist, she had no right to suppose that Gillian could not cope in an emergency and cope very efficiently, too. Just because she looked beautiful was no reason to suppose she was stupid or incapable. Gillian had not seemed either.

Mandy packed the last of Timmy's clothes and snapped down the lid of the shabby suitcase with a sigh. She was in no position to stand on her pride. She needed work and Jon was offering her a job. At least it would mean she would not be penniless over Christmas and for Timmy's sake she should accept Jon's offer even if it had been made out of charity.

'I'll make myself useful some way or another,' she vowed. 'And to Gillian, too.' She would, she resolved, make quite sure she earned whatever salary Jon intended to pay her. As to the future — when his own secretary returned, if she, Mandy, could prove her worth, she was sure Jon would find her another job and she'd make sure he could write her the very best of references with a good conscience.

Once again she found herself looking forward with eager enthusiasm to tomorrow and the new life she was to lead.

4

Jon looked up from his desk, his face white with exhaustion.

'How many still to come?' he asked Mandy.

'Only three more,' she told him with an anxious glance at the surgery clock. It was already a quarter past seven and she had not yet had a chance to nip upstairs and see if Timmy was asleep. As the evening surgery was from five-thirty to seven, she had adapted Timmy's routine so that she had him bathed, fed and tucked up in his cot before surgery started. Since this was almost an hour earlier than usual for him, she left the light on and a selection of toys in his cot until he felt sleepy enough to drop off.

For the first week she had been here Gillian had coped with the evening surgery; not, as Mandy believed, from any desire to assist her but because Jon had insisted it wasn't fair to expect Mandy to leave her child at his bedtime. Gillian had given in only because she was afraid Jon might change his mind about employing Mandy to work for him. It would have been typical of him to say the job was too much for her. But that danger was past. Mandy coped with quite astonishing efficiency and Jon had remarked that she was already as useful as Miss Hill, who had been with him since he bought the practice.

'Mandy is highly intelligent, more than willing and quick to grasp even the medical side, which must be very difficult for her,' he had told Gillian enthusiastically. 'It was a wonderful idea of yours to get her here, darling. I'm most grateful!'

Gillian had seen her chance to opt out entirely from an involvement in Jon's work.

'I'm so glad, Jon,' she had said pleasantly. 'It's such a relief to me, as well as to you. I promised Patty ages ago that I'd give her a hand tomorrow night. She's throwing a party — a kind of semi-business affair for clients — and she desperately wanted me to help her. As I promised, I hate to let her down. I had a word with Mandy at lunchtime and she said she could easily manage evening surgery, but I was just a bit worried in case you felt she couldn't. Now I can go with an easy conscience.'

Jon frowned.

'She can cope all right. That's not the point. She has Timmy to put to bed and . . . '

'Mandy said she could deal with the kid beforehand,' Gillian broke in, her face hardening. 'There is no need for you to make difficulties, Jon. Besides, I've been tied to this house for two weeks and it doesn't seem to have occurred to you that I *need* a break. Surely that's one of the reasons we got Mandy here?'

Jon had stayed silent. Mandy was so anxious to oblige that he found himself wondering apprehensively if Gillian wasn't deliberately imposing on her good nature. He was having to watch that he, himself, did not do so. It would be all too easy to take advantage of her readiness to help no matter how late or how tired she was; very easy, especially when he was so busy he did not know where else to turn.

He waited for Mandy to bring in his next patient. She seemed to have a natural ability to get on well with children and adults alike, and an unusual ability to sort out the genuine from the hypochondriacs! Before bringing in the next patient she had said with a smile:

'It's old Mrs Kennedy. I had a word with her and I think all she really wants is a kind word and a bottle of something to cheer her up. She lives alone, and being Christmas time, she's feeling a bit neglected.'

Jon sighed. In the two weeks Gillian had been helping him he doubted if she had bothered to talk to any of his patients. She was cool, aloof and disinterested. Mandy seemed as if she actually cared and she was quite right about Mrs Kennedy. Physically there was nothing wrong with the old girl.

Somehow he coped with the remaining patients. When the last one left he sat back in his chair and closed his eyes. He felt his hands shaking and knew that if he didn't let up soon he was going to crack. The 'flu epidemic showed no signs of abating and he wasn't sure how long he could continue to cope under this kind of pressure.

When he opened his eyes it was to find Mandy standing by his desk with a cup of coffee in her hand.

'It'll probably spoil your dinner, but I thought you might feel like it!' she said smiling, and then as an afterthought: 'Or would you rather have a whisky?'

Jon smiled back.

'No, your diagnosis is perfectly correct, Mandy. I think a whisky when I'm as tired as this would make me quite drunk. Coffee is the perfect stimulant and to hell with dinner!'

'I'm going up to look in on Timmy and then I'll be back and clear everything up,' she told him.

Jon looked at her searchingly.

'You must be exhausted, too,' he said with some concern. 'I'm afraid you've really been plunged in at the deep end, Mandy. You're coping marvellously. I'm very grateful.'

Tired though she was, she gave him a quick smile.

'I'm glad,' she said simply. 'As a matter of fact, you can't know how pleased I am. When Gillian phoned me about the job I was afraid you were just being charitable because you knew I was desperate for work. Now I've been here long enough to feel you really do need me. So, you see, I've nothing to complain about.'

Jon was surprised. He had had no idea how proud she was. He felt himself relax and some of the tiredness left him.

'I'll come up with you and see Timmy, may I?' he suggested. 'I've hardly had time to see him since you arrived and I'd like to, if you don't think it'll disturb him.'

Mandy nodded happily. Timmy looked his best in his little blue nightsuit, his face rosy from his bath and clean, for once! He had taken the move remarkably well, quite indifferent, it seemed, to the new faces and surroundings. How lucky she was that he was such an easy child. So far, Gillian and Jon had no reason to complain that he was disturbing the household with fractious crying or wakeful nights. He was happy in the new day nursery, too.

To Jon's disappointment the little boy was asleep when they entered Mandy's room. His little pyjama-clad bottom stuck in the air, his face buried in the fur of a large teddy-bear, there was not a great deal to be seen of him. Unwanted playthings lay in scattered heaps on the floor beneath the cot and Mandy looked apologetic.

'I'm afraid the room looks a bit of a

mess!' she said, 'but there just hasn't been time this evening to tidy it up. I hope Gillian didn't see it like this before she went out. She had the room looking so beautiful when I arrived!'

Jon grinned.

'It looks okay to me — just the way a nursery should look. I never did care for the spare room as it used to be — unlived in and impersonal.'

'You're very kind!' Mandy said impulsively. It was true, too. No wonder Jon was such a popular doctor. He was warm, sensitive, understanding and conscientious almost to a fault.

She tidied the room whilst Jon stood watching her, his face suddenly tired and sad.

'Gillian doesn't want a baby yet awhile,' he said, as much to himself as to her. 'I suppose a child does tie you terribly. I'm not as sympathetic as I ought to be about it because I'm tied anyway to my work here, so I thought . . . ' He broke off and then added quickly: 'But we will have children eventually . . . '

His voice trailed off uncertainly, as if even he did not quite believe in that eventuality. Mandy felt strangely uneasy. Jon had given her a glimpse into the more intimate side of his marriage. She felt intensely sorry for him, but knew this was not the time to say so. Instead she shrugged her shoulders casually, saying:

'Lots of girls don't feel ready for maternity until they have been married for some time. I expect I might have felt the same way, only I didn't exactly have a choice!'

Jon looked at her curiously.

'Do you really mean that, Mandy? Somehow you strike me as being a born mother, if there is such a thing. I've often thought there could be something in the theory that unmarried girls who get pregnant by mistake in fact subconsciously want a baby. I know it isn't really my business to ask you this, but how did you feel when you knew you were going to have Pete's child?

Appalled, or pleased?'

Mandy folded Timmy's dressing gown and paused as she laid it on the chair beside his cot, staring down at the sleeping child, her face soft and strangely beautiful as she sought for a truthful answer to Jon's question.

'If I'm honest I must admit I was pleased — at first, anyway. I loved Pete and I was thrilled to think I was actually carrying inside me a little living part of him. It was only later, when I told my parents and they were horrified, that I realised how wrong it was to be having a baby. I think I went through stages of being glad and sorry — glad for myself and sad for my parents.'

'It must have been tough for you!' Jon said. 'Do you think your parents will relent one day?'

Mandy shrugged.

'I don't know. It's Dad who objects more than Mother. But you have to try and see it from his point of view. He's a much respected bank manager in one of the Enfield branches and you know what people are like in the suburbs — very conventional and strait-laced — and Dad had to work hard all his life to get where he is. I disgraced him — or would do if anyone knew I had an illegitimate child. Mother understandably backs him up, although I know when Timmy was being born she wanted to be with me. Matron said she telephoned three times to ask how I was. Perhaps one day — if I get married — they'll own me again. I hope so!'

'I'm sure that day won't be far off,' Jon said truthfully. 'You're a very attractive girl, and I'll always think Pete was a lucky young devil to have known you. I loved him the same as you did, but I know in my heart he didn't really deserve you. He was a self-centred, irresponsible, feckless kid — always was. One forgave him because he was charming and . . . well, lovable. My parents spoilt him, of course. Do you miss him very much?'

She returned his gaze steadily.

'I miss not having a father for

86

Timmy. I miss not having someone to look after me when things are tough. But in a funny way it's almost as if Pete were a part of a dream. We were together such a short while! I even found myself forgetting what he looked like. I don't think I ever really knew him very well — or he me. We were too busy living and having fun together to take time to get to know one another. I'm not even sure if our marriage would have worked out, if we were really suited to one another. If Pete was irresponsible, I must have been, too.'

'You were very young, Mandy. One doesn't take life seriously in one's teens!'

Mandy smiled.

'There you are being kind again, finding excuses for me. I was as much to blame for what happened as Pete and that's all there is to it.'

'But you were the one left to pay the price — a pretty devastating price to pay, too. I admire you.'

'Then the feeling is mutual,' Mandy

said. 'I've never known anyone work as hard as you do. And I'm sure it's high time you had a meal and sat down and rested. I'll nip down and straighten up the surgery and then I'll get the supper. Gillian has left a casserole in the oven, so I've only to put it on the table. You go and watch telly or read the paper or something. I won't be long.'

Jon did as he was told. It was good to have even the smallest decision taken off his shoulders. He did not know if he had ever before in his life felt so tired, not even when he'd sat up all night as a student swotting before an exam.

When Mandy came into the drawing room to tell him supper was on the table he was fast asleep. She hesitated, unsure whether he needed the sleep more than the food. Finally she woke him and was glad that she had done so for he ate ravenously, despite the fact that Gillian's cooking was far from perfect. After they had eaten he insisted upon helping her to wash the dishes and made her sit down whilst he brewed the coffee.

It had been Mandy's habit to go to her own room after dinner in order not to intrude on Jon's and Gillian's rare moments alone together, but tonight, with Gillian away, it seemed kinder to stay. Jon was unusually talkative and she felt instinctively that he needed a listener. His remarks were all about Gillian — how she had looked the first time he'd set eyes on her; how he had decided there and then that this was the girl he wanted to marry. It had seemed a hopeless, impossible dream which could never materialise. Gillian had a dozen or more boyfriends, rich and with all the time in the world to give her. He still found it hard to believe that she had finally chosen him.

'She gave up a great deal when she married me,' he told Mandy thoughtfully. 'Her father understandably wanted her to marry someone who could give her the kind of life she had been used to. Gilly knew he was going to cut off her allowance, yet she married me in spite of everything. Sometimes I feel horribly guilty. Her life with me must be desperately boring and I simply can't afford to give her the kind of things she used to take for granted — holidays abroad, a decent car, servants and so on.'

'But she does have beautiful clothes!' Mandy burst out impulsively. 'You've been very generous in that way.'

Jon's face twisted in a way that showed his hurt.

'I don't give her a dress allowance. Her father relented enough to do that. Gilly has her own bank account which covers her clothes. She dresses so well, don't you agree, Mandy? She always looks beautiful.'

Mandy nodded. She had yet to see Gilly look other than as if she had stepped off a magazine cover. It took time, of course. Mandy knew that most of Gillian's morning was spent attending to her makeup, her hair, nails. She was fortunate in having a daily woman who came in to clean the house — at least Jon gave her that.

'It isn't much really,' Jon said. 'I'm hoping next year we can afford a cook-housekeeper. Gilly loathes cooking and we both resent the time she has to spend in the evening washing up and the like. We have so little time together and there isn't a thing I can do about it. It's a wonder she doesn't complain, being alone so much.'

Mandy remained silent. Gillian might not complain to Jon, but she never missed an opportunity to grumble to Mandy about the boredom and drudgery of being a doctor's wife. It made her uncomfortable to remember how grudgingly Gillian spoke of Jon whilst listening to him saying only the nicest things about her.

Unwilling though she was to admit it even to herself, Mandy knew that Gillian was utterly spoilt and terribly selfish. Any hopes she had had that they might become close friends had been dispersed after the first few days. Gillian was no more interested in her,

Mandy, than she was in Timmy, except for their usefulness to Jon. The welcome she had received she now knew to have sprung from Gillian's relief at being free from doing Miss Hill's job herself. Mandy did not resent this on her own behalf as much as on Jon's. When he was half killing himself to meet his obligations to his patients he should have been able to count on his wife's support.

'I hope Gilly's having a good party tonight!' Jon said, as much to himself as to Mandy. 'She deserves a break. I ought to be with her. I should have made the effort.'

Mandy did not question the meaning behind that remark. She supposed he was feeling guilty because he had not joined the party after surgery ended, yet anyone could see that he was in no fit state to go out. He was half asleep where he sat.

'I think an early night is indicated,' she said. 'I'm tired and I'm sure you are.'

Jon hesitated. He'd meant to sit up and wait for Gillian, but on the face of it this was senseless. She might be late and, as Mandy had said, he was hardly able to stay awake.

'Okay, Nurse. Bedtime it is!' he agreed, grinning. 'And thanks again, Mandy, for all your hard work. You've been an enormous help and I mean it.'

Mandy said good night and went into the kitchen to fill her hot-water bottle. She felt very contented. She knew Jon's compliment was genuine and knew that it was deserved. She was on top of the job and even able on occasions to take a tiny speck of the load off Jon's shoulders. Given a few more weeks.

But here she had to pull herself up. With Miss Hill due to return after the New Year, there might not be a few more weeks.

Her happiness, so unexpected, evaporated. She had been too busy and engrossed to consider the future, yet she must do so. She would shortly have to leave this house and make another life with Timmy elsewhere.

The thought was oddly distressing. In one short week she had come to look on this house as home, Jon as part of her family, his work as her work.

The hot-water bottle lay against her stomach as she paused uncertainly, her hand on the light switch. She was, she told herself fiercely, becoming a lot too dependent on Jon. Just because he was Pete's brother she had no right to consider him a relative, a kind of replacement father for her little son. He loved children and wanted one of his own. If only . . .

She pulled herself up sharply. This was no way to be thinking. Jon was a married man, deeply in love with his wife. He could never be anything more than an employer — or perhaps a favourite uncle. She had no claim on him, now or ever.

As she went upstairs to bed she thought wryly that she had never felt so lonely or so alone as she did now she was no longer living in an emotional vacuum. She told herself that Jon's occasional physical likeness to Pete was probably unsettling her, bringing back memories of a life she'd put firmly in her past and half forgotten. It had made her aware of her single state. If she wasn't careful she would soon be envying Gillian her right to sit on the other side of the fireplace, opposite Jon, in contented domestic intimacy. Or, worse still, find herself wishing that Gillian's beautiful bedroom and romantic négligé draped across the bed belonged to her, Mandy; that it was her bed, her husband waiting to make love to her.

Horrified at the turn her thoughts had taken, Mandy sought distraction in the child. Deliberately she woke him as she lifted him out of the cot and cradled him against her. He opened his eyes and gave a sleep-drugged smile. Her heart turned over. It wasn't Pete's eyes looking up at her drowsily, but Jon's. It was as if the two brothers had become confused in her mind and this child she held in her arms was Jon's child — the one he wanted; the one his wife had refused to give him.

She put Timmy hurriedly back in his cot where he fell instantly asleep. Her confusion turned to a dislike for herself. What kind of woman was she, wishing herself in another woman's shoes — no, in another woman's bed, envying her the husband she did not have!

Thank God nobody knows what I'm thinking, she told herself shakily. Next thing I'll be imagining I'm in love with Jon!

The frightening thing was that the thought did not seem particularly ludicrous nor even impossible. She climbed into bed and tried not to believe that it was all too probably true.

5

The party was in full swing. As always at the Sinclairs' house, drink was flowing freely. Pop music blared at full volume from the record player and an occasional couple danced. Someone had broken a glass and nobody had bothered to sweep up the fragments. Someone else had turned off the lights. In the big drawing room, gay with Christmas decorations, only the tree lights glowed.

Geoff's arms tightened around Gillian. She was wearing a clinging silk jersey trouser suit, the tunic cut low, the material outlining every curve of her body. She looked stunning and was well aware of it.

'You know I want to make love to you, don't you?' he whispered against her ear.

Gillian laughed.

'Of course. But you're not going to, darling. Believe it or not, I'm the faithful type!'

Geoff tightened his hold still further.

'But I don't believe it. You're far too lovely to belong to one man and one only. Anyway, I'm sure your husband doesn't appreciate you!'

Gillian laughed.

'On the contrary. Jon's still as crazy about me as he was on the day he married me. I'm afraid I'm not sex starved, Geoff, even if you'd like to think so.'

'No, I don't suppose you are!' Geoff said gloomily. He was a bit tight, but not more so than Gillian. The atmosphere all round was amorous and Gillian was driving him crazy, encouraging him one moment and denying him the next. 'You're a tantalising little bitch, Gillian,' he said, half angrily, half affectionately. 'God knows why Jon trusts you out alone at a party like this. I wouldn't if I were he.'

Gillian moved seductively against

him, amused to know the power she had over him.

'Jon knows I don't *need* another man,' she said pointedly. 'So why shouldn't he trust me?'

'Needing is different to wanting!' Geoff replied. 'Don't you want me just one little bit, Gilly?'

She shrugged indifferently.

'Perhaps I do; I'm not made of stone. You're a very attractive man, Geoff. And so is Mike. I love you both dearly.'

'Oh, shut up!' Geoff said angrily. 'If you think I'm going to be jealous of Mike, you're mistaken.'

'Aren't you then? Just a little tiny bit?' She mimicked his voice. 'Mike's jealous of you. He said so the last dance I had with him. He said he thought I preferred you to him.'

'Gilly, darling, *do* you?' Geoff asked eagerly, falling for the bait. 'I'm madly in love with you, you know that. If you'd just let me kiss you once I'd show you.'

'All right. Kiss me once and show

me!' Gillian said. 'But not in here. I'm The Doctor's Wife, don't forget, and my reputation is frantically precious.'

She allowed him to lead her out into the hall. Several couples were lying on the darkened stairway and the party seemed to have reached the pitch where anything was in order. She glimpsed Mike halfway up the stairs embracing a plump blonde girl she knew only as Janet, and her playful mood evaporated. Mike was supposed to be in love with her, or so he said. It was obvious he wasn't exactly pining over her refusal to go up to the spare room with him.

Her hand tightened on Geoff's arm.

'Do you really want me that badly?' she asked softly.

'You know I do!' His voice was shaky and satisfyingly genuine. Gillian led the way up to the spare room. It was empty. She lay down on the bed and Geoff half fell on top of her.

'Remember, one kiss only!' she said, as his mouth came down on hers and his hands reached out for her body.

She had, until now, been completely in control of herself; playing with Geoff's passion, unmoved by it but amused by it. She intended only to fool around for a while until he was half crazy with longing for her and then she would call a halt. She had never yet been unfaithful to Jon and had spoken the truth when she'd told Geoff she'd felt no need. But now the combination of alcohol and Geoff's urgent insistence began to weaken her armour of indifference. It was exciting to feel other arms than Jon's around her, other hands than his touching her. Jon was gentle and patient, but Geoff was violent and no longer in control of himself. Her body caught fire from his.

Jon would kill me if he knew, she thought, as Geoff began to tear off her clothes, oblivious now to her half-hearted protests. But Jon need never know, came the next thought. Besides, I need a little fun. Life's been dead lately. Then she surrendered to Geoff's determined demands and in a few minutes it was all over.

She was suddenly sober. Geoff lay breathing deeply beside her. She wasn't sure if he had passed out or was asleep. She edged away from him, trying to tidy herself up. She felt uneasy. It was a mad and stupid thing to have done. Geoff wasn't all that drunk and might be indiscreet. How often had she sat listening, amused by Mike and Geoff's cruel but often funny exchanges of gossip about this girl or that whose favours they had enjoyed. She had never meant to put herself into that category. Until now the two brothers had held her in a certain amount of awe; had shown respect for her even in their incessant flirtation. She sensed that it was not past either of them to have a bet as to who would take her first, neither really believing she was to be had. Now she'd let Geoff make love to her in a stupid moment of weakness that could have serious overtones if he talked about it and somehow it got back to Jon. Jon would be shocked and horrified. In a way she could understand how someone as serious and dedicated as Jon would see her adultery as unforgivable. In her own view it was really rather ridiculous in this permissive day and age to expect two human beings to be totally faithful all their lives. Change was sometimes necessary — even a good thing for a marriage. But she knew Jon would not share that view. Nor, she thought soberly, would her father. On her pre-wedding night he'd come into her room and lectured her, nearly succeeded in frightening her off the wedding.

'You've never taken anything very seriously in the whole of your life, Gilly,' he said. 'So I thought it about time I made it clear to you that some things are serious — marriage for one. What you did before was your own affair and I've never interfered with you. But after your marriage — that's another thing. Jon isn't the kind of young man who will tolerate loose living. He really loves you and that means he'll want you for himself. When you marry him, Gilly, you're agreeing to accept his terms. It's not too late to call the wedding off if you don't like those terms. Better to hurt the poor devil now than later. So think well about it. I'll cancel the whole thing even at this late hour if you want me to. What's it to be?'

She'd laughed, believing he was making a last attempt to put her off marrying Jon.

'Just because he hasn't any money . . .' she had begun to argue, but he'd cut her short.

'I'm not joking now, Gillian. You may think I've been an easy-going father, spoiling you the way I have and letting you have your own way. Maybe it's true. I believe in letting youth have its head. God knows one isn't young long. It's true I don't want you marrying Jon. I don't think you're right for him and he certainly has not the means to support you the way you want. But that's beside the point. The boy loves you — really loves you. Unless you're prepared to love him the same way, you're cheating him, and yourself, and I don't go along with that. I've played square all my life and I won't condone my own daughter treating marriage as an amusing game to be cast aside when the novelty wears off. Do you understand me, Gilly? If you're not sure you can keep to the rules, call it off now. I'll make it easy for you.'

'Do stop it, Father!' she said. 'Of course I'm in love with Jon. As to keeping to the rules and staying faithful to him, I'll put your mind at rest. We are perfectly suited in bed. That being the case, why should I want anyone else? Why else should I be so crazy keen to marry him?'

'For one thing, because you knew he would disappear from your life if you did refuse to marry him. For another, because I'd said no. For another, because you're bored with all the other young men hanging around at the moment and because you're looking for a new experience. There are a dozen reasons, Gilly, and I know them even if you do not. They aren't good reasons for marriage, either. Marriage isn't easy — not for anyone, and for two young people as ill-suited as you and Jon . . . '

'I am marrying him, Father, no matter what you say!'

No, there would be no quarter from her father if *he* ever found out she was fooling around with another man. She must indeed have been mad. Geoff wasn't worth the risk. Attractive and amusing though he was, she was not even mildly in love with him. Of the two brothers, she was far more attracted to the stronger character, Mike.

Damn Mike, she thought. It was his fault she was up here with Geoff. If he hadn't insulted her by consoling himself with that stupid fat blonde girl on the stair . . .

'Gilly, darling, are you awake?'

Geoff's voice, befuddled and slurred, broke in on her thoughts.

'Yes, and in need of a drink!' she answered harshly. He put an arm round her, but she flung it off angrily.

'Stop pawing!' she said coldly, as she got up off the bed and dressed hurriedly.

'Oh, Gilly, don't be cross!' Geoff pleaded stupidly as he sat up trying to clear his head. Had they made love or had he only dreamt it? He knew he'd had too much to drink, but not that much. She had let him . . .

'I'm off!' Gilly's cold voice interrupted. 'I was mad to come up here in the first place.'

She went out of the room, slamming the door behind her. Patty was coming upstairs, her face smudged with lipstick, her eyes glazed. She giggled as she recognised her friend.

'Gilly, darling, are you going to the bathroom? I'm just going there to repair the ravages. Are you enjoying yourself? Who've you been with?'

Gilly stiffened as the older girl linked her arm through hers. Patty looked slovenly, almost sluttish. Gillian's fastidious nature recoiled. There were times, and this was one of them, when their new-found friendship rocked a little on its slender foundations. Gillian knew very well that if life in this small town had been even half amusing she would have had no time for the Sinclairs. Her father would have called them 'common' in his blunt way. The two brothers were shrewd and intelligent and had risen rapidly from positions of junior salesmen in a somewhat shady second-hand-car firm to owning their own business. Patty's husband, Jock, was the only genuine estate agent among them and it was his knowhow, combined with their selling ability, that was making the firm such a success. But they had no background or class and Patty, in particular, could be loud and irritatingly silly.

They made money quickly and spent it as quickly, with careless disregard for saving. It appealed to Gilly, who had, until her marriage, never had to consider the cost of what she wanted. She was drawn to the Sinclairs as much by this facet of the family make-up as by their incessant search for a good time. She'd been starved of 'a good time' for nearly two years and it was easy to overlook their various shortcomings, their occasional vulgarity and ostentation, when they were so much fun to be with.

Now, regretting her own behaviour with Geoff, she was disenchanted with the Sinclairs and with Patty.

'Mike's been looking for you, sweetie!' Patty said as they went into the bathroom. She was giggling stupidly. 'Some blonde got hold of him and wouldn't let go and Mike's fed to the teeth. He said if I saw you to ask you if you'd let him drive you home. But you don't want to go yet, do you, luv? It's only one o'clock!'

Gillian washed her hands and dried them carefully on a none-too-clean towel.

'I do have to go. Jon may be waiting

up. I'll find Mike and tell him I'd like the lift. Super party, Patty. Thanks a lot!'

She hurried downstairs, feeling a little sick. In every way she had been stupid this evening. If she had not been so precipitate she could have had Mike rather than Geoff and now . . . now the evening was ruined.

She found Mike in the hall. He sounded moderately sober as he said:

'I've been searching the damned place for you, Gilly. Where were you hiding? Are you going to let me drive you home?'

Gillian nodded.

'But only that, Mike. I'm too tired to fight off unwelcome advances.'

He grinned, linking his arm through hers and giving it a friendly squeeze.

'And who said I intended making any advances? Not that I wouldn't, given the slightest encouragement from you. You're the loveliest woman in this place, if not in any place,' he said, genuinely meaning it. 'It wouldn't be a bit difficult falling in love with you.'

Gillian felt herself softening towards him. It wasn't his fault Geoff was his brother and right now she was loathing him. Mike, the elder of the two, was far more mature; had a lot more to him than Geoff. She'd always preferred Mike and amused herself in duller moments imagining what an affair with him would be like. Not that she seriously intended becoming involved with him either.

In the car she said to Mike:

'Your brother got very drunk and somewhat amorous this evening. In fact, he was so tight I don't think he could distinguish truth from fiction.'

'Silly young fool!' Mike said indulgently. 'Hope he wasn't a bore to you, Gilly?'

She gave a casual laugh.

'Not really! I walked into the spare room and found him in bed with a girl and guess what! He was calling her Gilly! I might have been embarrassed if it hadn't struck me as funny.'

'Damn fool!' Mike said again. 'Still, I can't say I blame him for wanting you, darling. You really do drive a chap up the wall. Lucky husband waiting in bed for you to come back to him. Wish I were he.'

Happier now that she had covered herself against Geoff's possible boasts in the morning, Gillian leant against him.

'You say nice things and you're nice and I like you,' she said. 'So I'll return the compliment you paid just now and tell you I think you were the most attractive man at the party. If I weren't married . . . '

'Yes, that's the fly in the ointment, isn't it?' Mike broke in ruefully. 'Are you always going to be faithful to that doctor of yours, Gilly?'

'Probably. I don't know. I expect so.'

'I'm not so sure,' Mike said quietly. 'Somehow I don't think one man will ever be enough for you.'

Gillian remained silent. He obviously knew her better even than she knew herself; certainly better than Jon who trusted her absolutely. There was something in Mike that interested as well as attracted her. He knew and understood women and she felt it could be more than a little exciting to have such a man for a lover — if she ever decided to have a lover.

Mike was no he-man. Slim with narrow hips and small hands and feet, he might have seemed at first glance a little effeminate. But there was something essentially male about him, a hardness, a hint of cruelty about the mouth, a promise, a challenge in the eyes. Whatever the cause of it, Gillian recognised his appeal to women. No wonder he had been so successful as a salesman. She could imagine most women wanting to give him what he wanted — ready to buy what he had to sell.

They had come to the corner of the road down which lay Gillian's house. As Mike was negotiating the turn, there was a muted bang and the car lurched.

Mike jammed on the brakes and swore softly.

'Damnation!' he said. 'That's another tyre gone and I bloody well haven't got the spare back since I took a slow puncture in to be mended yesterday. What a sweat!'

Gillian laughed.

'And you an ex-car salesman!' she said.

Mike grinned back at her.

'There's one born every minute!' he said. 'I'll have to get a taxi back. Any phone boxes around here, Gilly?'

She shook her head.

'Not that I know of. You'd better come home with me and telephone from there.'

Mike nodded.

'Okay, I'll do just that. I *am* sorry, Gilly.'

'Forget it!' she told him. 'The house is only a few yards down the road.'

Mike locked the car and walked her home. The street was deserted and the house in darkness. Gillian found her key and unlocked the front door. She was reaching for the hall light when Mike, close behind her, stumbled over the umbrella stand and brought it crashing to the ground.

Gillian switched on the light and they stood staring at each other, shocked at the noise they had made in the silent house and hysterically near to laughter.

Mike had just begun a second apology when a light went on on the upstairs landing. Both of them supposed they had woken Jon, but when the figure moved into the light at the top of the stairs, Gillian breathed a sigh of relief. It was only Mandy.

'It's okay, Mandy,' she called softly. 'We knocked over the umbrella stand.'

Mandy stared down into the hall. She was still half asleep. Her hair fell across her face as she stood there, still a little frightened at the thought of intruders.

'You sure you're all right?' she called back.

'Yes! Go back to bed!' Gillian said.

Over her shoulder Mike stared up at

the girl on the landing. She looked about sixteen in her navy dressing gown, her soft fair hair in golden strands over her flushed cheeks, her eyes wide and a little scared. He knew who it must be. Gillian had told them all about Mandy and 'her illegit'. At the time he and Patty and Geoff had made a few lewd jokes about Jon's brother having it off and then popping off before he could be stung for maintenance. Now it didn't seem quite so funny. The girl was only a kid herself, looking anything but the type to fall into bed at the drop of a pin. If one word alone could describe her, innocence was the adjective that stood out in his mind.

They remained standing there until Mandy had returned to her room. Then Gillian nudged his arm.

'Get a move on, Mike,' she said. 'Next thing we'll be waking poor old Jon. The phone's in there!'

He went into the drawing room and dialled the all-night taxi service. While the number rang out, he found himself regretting the girl had not come downstairs so that he could have seen her closer to. The half-seen contours of her profile were tantalising his memory. He knew that she was not beautiful — not in the way Gillian was beautiful, yet the girl had some other quality he was not yet able to define — a softness, a femininity? He came back to the word innocence. Then a reply from the taxi service put her out of his mind.

Gillian brought him a drink and they sat in the drawing room waiting for the taxi to arrive. She seated herself on the arm of his chair and as he smiled up at her, she felt renewed chagrin at the memory of the interlude with Geoff. She hoped fervently that he wouldn't mention it to Mike, but she knew better than to count on his discretion. Geoff was a born boaster and her only hope of keeping Mike ignorant of the fact was her word against Geoff's.

'It was quite a party!' She chose her words carefully. 'I don't imagine your dear brother will remember much about it. He fairly put the drink away tonight.'

Mike grinned indulgently.

'Geoff's a fool. He's never had much of a head for it and doesn't know when to stop. All the same, from what you told me earlier, he didn't have enough to incapacitate him.'

'I wonder who the girl was!' Gillian said pointedly. 'The one he went to bed with.'

Mike shrugged. He was not interested in his brother's casual affairs.

'Does it matter?'

Gillian gave a careless laugh.

'Not to me. I've no designs on Geoff, much as I like him.' She ruffled Mike's hair, laughing again as she added: 'Now I might have cared if it had been *you*, Mike. I might even have felt the tiniest bit jealous.'

He looked up at her, puzzled. Gillian often flirted with him the same way she did with Geoff, but he'd never supposed she was seriously interested. Now he wondered. He was flattered and yet, to his own surprise, not particularly stirred by the knowledge that he'd made a possible conquest. Trying to analyse his reactions as the taxi drove him home, he realised that Gillian's major attraction for him had been her unobtainability. He was sick of lays; of sleeping with girls about whom he very often knew little more than their names. Women had always found him attractive and the novelty of quick easy conquests had long since worn off. Gillian, when his sister Patty had first introduced him, had struck him as being a cut above the average girl he picked up to satisfy his needs. Very attractive, very self-assured and, without doubt, very experienced, she was a challenge. That she had a singularly attractive husband added to the fun of the game of trying to make the grade with her.

Not, he thought wryly as he paid off the taxi driver and went into the house, that he would refuse to accommodate

Gilly if she were to make herself available. But a little of the gilt had gone off the gingerbread now he sensed she could be his for the asking.

Except for a few remaining guests lying in odd corners of the house, the party had ended. Mike had lost interest in it and, without looking for Patty or Geoff, he made his way up to bed. As he mounted the stairs he suddenly recalled the young girl on the landing in Gilly's house — the one called Mandy. He was intensely curious about her and that brief glimpse of her lingered in his mind, tantalising, unknown, unexplored. She didn't fit the picture Gillian had given him — of the kind of girl he knew only too well, sleeping around, having the best of the permissive society and then getting caught. The girl he had seen had struck him above all as innocent. Yet she couldn't be!

As he climbed into bed and closed his eyes, it was Mandy's face and not Gillian's which touched the edge of his dreams.

6

On Christmas Eve Jon went down with 'flu. By the time morning surgery was finished he knew he could not keep going any longer. His head was throbbing unbearably and when Mandy came in with coffee she found him slumped over his desk. His temperature when she took it was 104 degrees.

Somehow she managed to get him upstairs and on to his bed. Gillian was out at the hairdresser's and would not be back until lunchtime. Jon was only semi-coherent.

'Nothing to worry about. Just 'flu!' he told her, as she pulled the duvet over him. He mumbled something she could not understand and then said: 'Better phone Dr Harvey. Ask him if he could possibly take over for me.' His next words did not make sense and thoroughly frightened, Mandy ran down to the hall to telephone the elderly doctor, now retired, from whom Jon had bought the practice.

Dr Harvey was in his seventies and Mandy doubted very much whether he could possibly cope with the huge workload that was Jon's daily task whilst the epidemic raged. Small wonder Jon had fallen victim to 'flu. It did not surprise her in the least; he had worked himself to a pitch of exhaustion and his resistance must be lowered to the extreme.

The old doctor promised to come at once. Mandy paused before going back upstairs to see if there was anything she could do for Jon in the meanwhile. She was uncertain whether she should telephone the hairdresser and ask that Gillian be informed her husband was ill. The call seemed pointless on reflection. Gillian would be home anyway in half an hour. While these thoughts were passing through Mandy's mind, the phone suddenly rang. It was Mike, wanting to speak to Gillian.

Mandy explained the situation.

'I was about to invite Gillian out to lunch,' Mike said. 'But, obviously, under the circumstances . . . ' He broke off and then added: 'Is there anything I can do? It must be a bit worrying for you alone there and Jon ill.'

Mandy told him the doctor was coming and declined the offer of help.

'Thanks all the same!' she added genuinely. Although a useless suggestion, she really did appreciate the thought.

'Tell you what!' Mike said. 'I've nothing to do right now, so how about if I pop round to the hairdresser's and give Gillian a lift home? It'll save a bit of time, wouldn't it?'

Mandy thanked him again and as she went upstairs to Jon it crossed her mind that she may have misjudged Mike. From the little she had heard about the Sinclair family she had assumed she would not much like them. She knew that Jon did not care for them by the singular tone of voice he always used when talking about them to Gillian. Her sensitive ear had caught the note of disapproval which Gillian had either not heard or else chose to ignore.

She forgot all about Mike the moment she went back into the bedroom. Jon was delirious. His face was flushed with fever and he did not recognise her. As she bent over him, putting a hand to his forehead, he reached out and pulled her down to him, murmuring:

'Gilly! My head hurts. Darling, you do love me, don't you?'

Mandy felt her face flushing a deep scarlet as he rambled on. Her heart was thudding painfully and she tried to pull herself away from his embrace. He seemed to realise she was trying to escape, for he held her even more tightly and said hoarsely:

'We could have such beautiful children, you and I. Please, Gilly, *please*, darling . . . '

Mandy bit her lip so hard she felt the taste of blood. Her face now was chalk white, her whole body trembling, as she managed to ease herself away from his arms. He moaned softly and she turned her head away, appalled by her shattering emotions. With all her heart she longed to stay close to him, to take him in her arms and cradle his head against her; to say all the soothing words she would have spoken to Timmy had he been lying there helpless and ill; to Pete; to anyone she loved.

I love him! she thought with a terrible sense of despair. I love him, *I love him!*

She walked to the window and stared out into the barren garden. The scene was cold and wintry and gave her no comfort. Swinging round, she forced herself to look at the man on the bed. His eyes were closed now as he lay exhausted against the pillow. She felt a renewal of fear. Jon was obviously very ill. If only the doctor would come! This was a particularly virulent type of 'flu bug and several of Jon's patients, including her predecessor, Miss Hill, had developed pneumonia because they had not given in and sought treatment early enough. Jon might have been feeling ill for days and been too conscientious to say so, or to give way.

Suddenly she remembered the previous night; how totally whacked Jon had been and how Gillian, the wife who should have been home taking care of him, had arrived back so late from the Sinclairs' party where she'd been enjoying herself!

Mandy felt a moment of pure hatred for Gillian. Then checked herself quickly. She was letting her own feelings for Jon cloud her judgement. Gillian had a right to enjoy herself if she wished. She, Mandy, was paid to act as Jon's secretary-assistant. It was not Gillian's job to share Jon's work.

But even as she tried to excuse Gillian, Mandy knew that if she had been in Gillian's shoes she would never have gone off to a party without Jon, and particularly when he could have done with every little bit of help she could give. Her way of loving was very different from Gillian's. She would give up anything and everything for the man she loved — just as she had once given up everything for Pete.

The front-door bell rang, breaking into her thoughts. She ran downstairs and breathed a sigh of pure relief when she saw the elderly man standing there, his Gladstone bag in his hand.

As she took him upstairs, Mandy explained as briefly as she could the circumstances leading to Jon's collapse. It was only a matter of minutes before Dr Harvey confirmed her opinion.

'A nasty case of 'flu!' he said. 'I'll write a prescription, Nurse. Get him into bed as soon as possible and give him a tepid sponge bath to get the fever down.'

Mandy blinked nervously.

'I'm not a nurse,' she said apologetically. 'I'm a secretary, acting nurse, whilst Miss Hill is away in hospital.'

The old man looked at her quizzically.

'Well, do the best you can, young woman. He doesn't need special nursing,' he said. 'From what I hear, you're not likely to find the district nurse sitting at home twiddling her thumbs, so it's no use hoping she'll take over from you. Where's his wife? She'll have to look after her husband if you can't.'

'She will be back presently. Naturally I'll do anything I can. But what about the doctor's patients? He's been trying for several weeks to get a locum but . . . '

'I'll take over!' the old doctor said brusquely. 'I may be retired these past two years but I'm still quite capable, young lady.' He looked down at Jon and shook his head. 'Silly young pup — should have asked for my help weeks ago!'

Mandy felt her heart warming towards the old doctor. Jon had, in fact, considered asking Dr Harvey to step into the breach but not until he had to, which meant not until he felt he couldn't cope alone. Now that moment had definitely come and, as Dr Harvey had said, it was a pity he had not done so earlier.

'Well, get him into bed, young lady, and I'll come back after lunch and see who needs visiting. Nice Christmas we're going to have. I'll see myself out. Used to be my house, you know, so I know my way.'

He had barely left before Gillian returned with Mike. They came into the room together as Mandy was struggling to support Jon with one arm whilst she removed his shirt with the other.

Gillian looked shocked.

'I'd no idea he was ill!' she said helplessly. 'He seemed okay at breakfast. He looks ghastly!'

She made no move to help Mandy. It was Mike who went across to the bed and supported the semi-conscious man whilst Mandy undressed him. Gillian sounded frightened.

'Is he very bad, Mandy? I'm not good with sick people. I'm sorry, but I can't help. I've got a horror of illness. Is it 'flu? My God, I hope I don't catch it. I . . . '

It was Mike who interrupted her, saying:

'Why don't you go downstairs and get yourself a drink, Gillian. We can manage.'

'It's such a shock, seeing him so ill!' Gillian said weakly. 'Are you sure . . . ?'

'Quite sure!' Mike broke in. 'Beat it, Gillian!'

She did as she was told, grateful to be sent away.

'Bloody useless!' Mike muttered as he pulled on Jon's pyjama trousers. He glanced at Mandy and smiled: 'Damned difficult dressing someone else, especially if they're *non compos mentis!*'

Enormously grateful to have him there, Mandy smiled back.

'Sorry to be such a bother!' Jon said, suddenly coherent again. He attempted a smile at both of them and then whispered: 'My head hurts one hell of a lot!'

'Dr Harvey left a prescription!' Mandy said as she pulled the bed-clothes round Jon and settled him more comfortably against the pillows. 'I don't quite see how I can get out to get it. I've left Timmy — my little boy — at the day nursery and I should have fetched him half an hour ago.'

Mike put a reassuring hand on her arm.

'That's easily dealt with. We'll send Gillian up to sit with Jon and I'll drive you to the chemist's and the day nursery in my car. We can kill two birds with one stone.'

As they left the room Mike said:

'Gillian will just have to pull herself together. A phobia about illness is not very appropriate in a doctor's wife! No doubt a stiff drink will help her. Come along then, Mandy. Let's not waste any more time.'

Mandy went to collect her coat. Outside there was a bitter, northerly wind and she shivered as she climbed into Mike's car. He reached over to the

131

back seat and pulled a car rug over her knees.

'Better?' he asked solicitously. 'It's damn cold though I suppose it's seasonal. We might even get a white Christmas!'

Mandy felt herself relaxing. Only now did she realise how tightly strung her nerves had been. First, she had had two severe shocks — the finding of Jon collapsed over his chair and then the emotional shock of discovering that she loved him.

'I *am* grateful for all you're doing!' she said quickly to Mike, afraid to let her thoughts about Jon invade her.

'Glad to be of help, Mandy!' he replied, glancing down at her. Now that he had a chance to see her at close quarters, she looked older than the schoolgirl apparition he'd glimpsed on the stairs the previous night. But the delicate, pale, tense little face still held that same look that had haunted him ever since — of a purity and innocence so much at variance with the impression Gillian had given him of the girl. He was intensely curious about her. But he sensed that her mind was preoccupied and that this was no time to ask personal questions.

'Tough luck walking into this packet of trouble right at the start of your new job!' he said sympathetically. 'I gather you haven't been here very long. Gillian said you weren't a trained nurse, so I imagine you've not found it all that easy to cope.'

'There has been an awful lot to learn!' Mandy admitted. 'But I've been enjoying the work — until today. I've really felt I was doing something worth while. Jon was pretty desperate, what with the 'flu going round and Miss Hill away. He really needed someone experienced, I'm afraid. As it is, he's been over-working and now . . . '

Mike heard the tremble of her voice and felt a surge of protectiveness.

'Don't worry! He'll be okay!' he said. 'I just hope Gillian pulls herself together and does her share, though

I'm afraid she won't be much help!'

Loyalty forbade Mandy expressing the agreement she felt. Mike noticed the reticence and thought:

She could have been bitchy about Gillian. Lots of girls would have been. She's a nice kid! Gillian wouldn't have been so reticent.

His interest in Mandy took on a new turn when she collected her little boy from the nursery school. Suddenly she was no longer 'a nice kid' but very much a woman as she consoled her child for not being there to collect him on time. The boy snuggled against her as she talked to him in a soft, warm voice Mike had not heard her use before. He was intrigued. This maternal aspect of the girl was as unexpected as it was attractive. He found himself longing to hear her speak to him with that amount of tenderness and attention in her voice!

Steady, Mike! he told himself. If you aren't damn careful, you might find yourself falling in love with her!

The idea made him laugh as if he, Mike, could fall in love with anyone! He'd resolved years ago to enjoy women without any strings attached. Kiss and run. That was his motto. A bachelor's life was Mike Sinclair's ideal. It did not include falling in love.

Nevertheless, he was very much aware of Mandy as she sat beside him, nursing the child. On a sudden impulse he went into the toy shop adjoining the chemist's where he collected the prescription for Jon, and bought the boy a huge teddy bear.

'For Christmas!' he explained, depositing it on Mandy's lap.

Mandy was embarrassed by the extravagance of the gift. She looked at him shyly.

'You shouldn't . . . I mean, you ought not . . . there was no need . . . '

Mike grinned.

'Okay, so I shouldn't, I ought not and there was no need but I wanted to. Okay?'

Mandy let Timmy grab the bear from

her and pull it free from its cellophane covering. He was chattering excitedly. She relaxed, smiling.

'It was very kind!' she said. 'Timmy's obviously thrilled. All the same . . . '

'No more 'buts'. The deed is done and a happy Christmas to all!' Mike broke in, delighted as much by Mandy's confusion as by her gratitude. He remembered the bottle of perfume he'd bought for Gillian for Christmas and thought wryly:

She'll accept it with a casual 'Thanks, Mike'. It won't mean half as much as this present for the kid means to Mandy. Gilly's spoilt.

He decided not to give Gillian the perfume, after all. He'd noticed the Christmas tree in the hall of their house. He could easily tear the card with Gilly's name off the package, scribble Mandy's name on it and deposit it under the tree when he took her back. The idea pleased him enormously. He could imagine her surprise and confusion when she found it there. Gillian had told him Mandy was practically penniless. A luxury present like the expensive perfume he'd chosen for Gillian would be a big thrill. He would have enjoyed seeing her unwrap it!

I'll call round on Christmas morning, he thought. No reason why I shouldn't. I can be enquiring after Jon. Better get some flowers for Gilly while I think about it. I don't want to put her nose out of joint!

Mike let his imagination have free play until they reached the house. He got out to open the car door for Mandy and said reluctantly:

'I don't suppose there's much else I can do now, is there?' He helped her with the child. 'Promise you'll ring me if there's anything that crops up that I could do. Gillian has my number.'

'Yes, of course, and thank you again, for everything!' Mandy said warmly. 'You've been very kind!'

He watched her go indoors with a curious sense of loss. He would like to have gone in with her, but he didn't feel like facing Gillian. Unusual for him, he wanted to be alone. He didn't want the company of Patty or Geoff either. He decided to stop at a pub for lunch instead of going home. He needed a drink — and time to sort out the strange new feelings that were rapidly taking control of him.

Gillian came running downstaris to meet Mandy. She looked flushed and angry.

'You've been absolutely *ages!*' she complained. 'Whatever were you . . . ?' She caught sight of the teddy bear Timmy was clutching to him and stared at Mandy's embarrassed face. 'You've been Christmas shopping!' she said indignantly. 'And there's poor Jon deathly ill . . . '

'Mike bought the teddy bear at the shop next to the chemist's!' Mandy broke in. 'It took a minute. We were as quick as possible. Is Jon worse?'

'How the hell should I know!' Gillian said furiously. 'He's delirious. I thought you were supposed to give him a tepid bath. Isn't that what Dr Harvey said?'

Mandy felt her cheeks burning.

'I thought you'd do that!' she said quietly. 'I'm not a nurse, Gillian. I . . . '

'Well, for heaven's sake, Mandy, nor am I! I don't see why *you* can't nurse Jon. You know how I am with sick people. If you can't cope, I'll have to get a private nurse, no matter what it costs.'

Her tone had become wheedling as she sensed Mandy's reluctance to take on nursing duties.

'Surely you can cope?' she said again. 'I know you've a lot to do but I'll make it up to you, I promise. Please, Mandy. It really does upset me to see Jon so ill. Can't you look after him?'

It was on the tip of Mandy's tongue to cry out: 'Yes, of course. I want to take care of him. But you're his wife and I'm a stranger.'

She bit back the words. How could she possibly explain to Jon's wife that she was the very last person who should be caring for Jon. That she should stay as far away as possible from him, lest she should find herself falling even more deeply and hopelessly in love with him. If Gillian knew . . . But she did not know and there was no way of explaining.

'Yes, I'll look after him,' she said quietly. 'Do you think you could give Timmy his lunch? It's long overdue!'

'I suppose so. I've seen you do it often enough. Thank goodness he feeds himself!'

Mandy found herself smiling. Poor Gillian — with Timmy the choice of two evils.

'I'll leave him with you, then,' she said, and went upstairs to minister to Jon.

Surprising herself, Mandy found she was able to assume the rôle of nurse without difficulty. Jon ceased to be Jon, but became a patient as she gently sponged his body with tepid water until gradually the intense heat of his body was reduced.

It was only later when she was sitting

in the chair by his bed, and he suddenly opened his eyes and spoke, that she was fully aware of him again.

'I feel so much better!' he said coherently — even managing a smile. 'Thanks, no doubt, to you, Mandy. Sorry to be such a nuisance.'

She smiled back at him reassuringly as she strove to keep the relief and happiness from her eyes.

'I was sitting here wondering how to give you your medicine,' she said in as flippant a voice as she could manage. 'I was afraid if I poured it down your throat you might choke. Can you sit up a bit if I help you and swallow it?'

She put her arm round him and for a moment felt the weight of his head against her. Her newly discovered love for him welled through her being with even greater force.

It's only because he is Pete's brother, she told herself in a desperate effort not to reveal her feelings. He means nothing to me, nothing at all!

'Gillian is downstairs. I'll call her!'

she said, taking the medicine glass from him and moving quickly from the bed. 'She'll be so relieved you're better.'

'Don't go for a minute, Mandy!' Jon called weakly. 'I want to know what's happening. What time is it? What about my visits to patients?'

'You're not to worry!' Mandy said firmly. 'Dr Harvey is taking over until you are better. He'll see to everything. All you've got to do is rest and get well again.'

'There's the Fergusson baby due any moment. If . . . '

'Don't think about anything but getting well,' Mandy interrupted. 'I'll see Dr Harvey has all the information he needs. If necessary, I'll deliver the Fergusson baby myself.'

Jon lay back on the pillows, smiling.

'You probably would at that. You're quite a girl, Mandy. Somehow I know I needn't worry; that I can trust you. Whether poor old Dr Harvey can be trusted is another matter. What do you think?'

'I'm sure he'll manage!' Mandy said reassuringly. 'Anyway, you'll be back in harness in a day or two — but only if you rest now you've got the chance. I'll send Gillian up, shall I?'

She escaped from the room and, closing the door behind her, leaned against it drawing a deep breath. She was shocked at her own weakness. All the time she had stood there, answering him calmly and impersonally, she had been longing to kneel by the bed and say: 'Don't worry. I'll take care of you. I love you. I love you.'

Instead it would be Gillian who held his hand and stroked his forehead until he fell asleep.

Angry and ashamed at such thoughts, Mandy hurried down to the kitchen. Timmy was in his high chair and most of his lunch was strewn over the floor. Gillian looked harassed.

'Thank goodness you're here. I don't seem to be coping very well!' she said.

'Jon wants you. He's better, but fussing about his work. Perhaps you could get him to sleep.'

Mandy knew her voice was terse, but she could not speak normally. Avoiding Gillian's eyes, she began to tidy the mess Timmy had made. Gillian remained sitting. She said weakly:

'I suppose I'll have to go up. I don't want to.'

When Mandy did not reply, Gillian stood up and, shrugging helplessly, walked out of the room.

As Gillian passed the Christmas tree in the hall she gave a deep sigh. Some Christmas this was turning out to be, she thought. Trust Jon to choose a moment like this to get the 'flu. She wished she need not go into the sickroom. Mandy didn't seem to be scared, but she, Gillian, had no wish to be near any germs that she might catch. She was afraid of illness. She could still remember the smell of the hospital where she'd been taken to see her dying mother. The phobia, beginning then, had increased with the years. Since neither she nor her father were ever ill, she'd not realised how the obsession had developed and consolidated in her mind until after she had married Jon. Then, the smell of the surgery or even the brief hint of antiseptic about his person brought back the old feeling of revulsion. She had always insisted that Jon bathed and changed his clothes after work. Unless he did so she could not bear him to come near her. The week she had had to assist him in the surgery had been a nightmare.

She knew she should never have married a doctor. Not long after they were married she had had to explain to Jon why she turned away from his embrace so violently when he came in from work. She had told him their marriage was a mistake, that it could never work because of the way she felt. Jon had been wonderfully patient and understanding.

'You're my wife and you're staying that way, Gilly!' he had said. 'I married you because I love you, not because I wanted you to share my work. I still love you and want you and need you. Naturally I'm sorry you feel as you do but I realise you can't help it and I'll never hold it against you. As far as possible, I'll keep my working life apart from you.'

He had kept his promise — until the unfortunate Miss Hill had fallen ill and she had been forced to step into the breach. Only Jon knew what an effort of will had been required to attend those ghastly surgeries. She'd needed several pretty strong drinks before and after each one to survive them. Now Jon was ill and it was obvious Mandy expected her to look after him. Would Jon expect it, too?

She went into the room hesitantly. Jon was lying in bed with nothing to show he was ill except for the medicine bottle on the bedside table. He opened his eyes and saw her.

'Gilly! Hullo, darling! Sorry if I frightened you.'

His voice was normal — no trace of that weird unnatural delirium that had so unnerved her earlier.

She forced herself to approach the bed.

'Are you feeling better?' she asked.

He reached out to take her hand. She steeled herself not to withdraw it.

'Much better. Sorry I gave you a scare, darling. Being a bit of a nuisance, aren't I?'

'It's okay!' she said, withdrawing her hand. She was conscious now of a faint smell of antiseptic. 'Is it all right if I smoke?'

'Yes, of course.'

He watched her as she lit a cigarette. Her hair was newly coiffured and she was beautifully made up as always. She looked very lovely: fresh, cool, beautiful. Her hand, faultlessly manicured and very smooth and white, toyed with the cigarette. He wished she would touch his forehead which throbbed and ached with the fever. He would have liked to close his eyes and go to sleep with her cool, soft hand against his cheek. But he would not ask. Sick as he was, knowing her aversion to illness and therefore to himself, he understood that she could not bring herself voluntarily to touch him. The thought saddened him. He loved her very much and because he felt so weak he needed the comfort her hands could give him.

Somewhere in the haziness of his mind he seemed to remember the cool touch of her hands undressing him and, later, gently sponging his body, drying and powdering him.

'You've been marvellous!' he said softly. 'I feel so much better, Gilly. Thank you, darling, for taking such good care of me.'

Not knowing what he was thinking, Gillian supposed he was becoming delirious again. Quickly she stood up and said:

'I wish I could stay longer, but I've things I must see to, Jon. I'll come back later.'

He frowned.

'I don't know if you should, Gilly. This 'flu's damnably infectious. You ought to stay away from me, darling, or you'll go down with it.'

She stared at him from large frightened eyes. She might already have breathed in a germ.

'Better move into the other spare room for a few days,' Jon was saying. 'I'd be the one to move out, but . . . '

'That's all right, I'll go,' Gillian broke in. She began feverishly to gather up her vast collection of beauty preparations from the dressing table. She tipped over a bottle of her favourite perfume, but in her now frantic haste to be out of the germ-laden room she did not stop to mop it up. The air became filled with the scent of Arpège. She did not stop to collect her clothes. Mandy could fetch anything else she wanted later. For the moment she had no other thought in her mind but to escape. It was fortunate that Jon's eyes had closed and he was too nearly asleep to realise that she had left the room without even a glance at him, let alone a goodbye.

7

'Thank God you're here, Mike!' Gillian said as she moved restlessly round the drawing room chain-smoking. 'I don't know when I've ever been so bored on a Christmas Day.'

Mike looked up from the floor where he lay full length building towers of bricks for Mandy's little boy to knock down again. He was quite enjoying himself, a fact which he guessed was annoying Gillian, who wanted his attention centred on herself.

He had come to the house after lunch in order to see Mandy. Gillian had opened the door to him and assumed, understandably enough, that he'd come to see her. To Mike's amusement, she'd been baby-minding young Timmy as Mandy was trying to catch up with the paper-work left over since last night's surgery. From what he could gather, the poor girl was up to her eyes in it, nursing Jon, helping Dr Harvey and trying to mind her own child as well. Yet Gillian had complained bitterly because she had had to cook the Christmas lunch with no Mandy to assist her.

'I wish we could go out somewhere!' Gillian said fretfully. 'If only we didn't have this damned kid on our hands!'

'He's rather fun!' Mike said truthfully. Children were a novelty to him and Timmy was the first baby he'd ever got down on his hands and knees and played games with. He'd not the slightest wish to go pub-crawling with Gilly. He was quite content waiting for Mandy to appear. Sooner or later she would have to come for the child.

'Can't you think of *anything* to do, Mike?' Gillian asked petulantly. She switched on the television and turned it off in disgust at finding a pantomime on one channel and a circus on the other. 'I suppose we could play gin rummy!'

Mike did not bother to reply as he started a fresh column of bricks for the child. Gillian felt exasperated. She was bored and yet, at the same time, strangely excited. Mike attracted her far more than she had previously realised. It wasn't simply a physical attraction. His personality seemed to have changed indefinably these last few days. He was as friendly as ever, yet somehow remote. It was as if he were challenging her; if not deliberately then unconsciously. She wanted him to notice her now in a way she'd never bothered about when he had been aware of her.

Gillian was nearer the truth than she realised. Mike had, in fact, changed a great deal very suddenly, and most of all in his attitude to her. Until he'd met Mandy he'd been conscious of Gillian as a highly attractive and desirable woman with whom he would certainly have had an affair if she'd been willing. Now he was no longer in the least concerned with her. He had thoughts for no one but Mandy and it was this very disinterest in Gillian that had aroused her interest in him. As she watched him amusing himself with the child, she couldn't understand why, since he had supposedly come to spend the afternoon with her, he was making no move to flirt with her in his usual manner whenever the chance arose.

'You're a strange guy, Mike!' she said. 'I don't know if I altogether understand you. I never realised you actually liked kids.'

He grinned up at her.

'Still waters!' he said. 'Anyway, you know the old saying, Gilly: 'All the world is queer save thee and me, and even thee's a little queer!' You're a bit odd, too, if I may say so.'

Gillian was happy to have the conversation centred on herself.

'In what way?' she asked curiously.

'Oh, I don't know. Take that 'thing' you've got about sickrooms. I imagine Jon's feeling a bit neglected, isn't he? Shouldn't you be up there with him?'

Gillian frowned.

'Heavens, no. Mandy's being the ministering angel. Anyway, Jon doesn't want me to risk catching the 'flu.'

Mike's smile vanished.

'That's all very well, but *you're* his wife, Gilly.'

Gillian laughed but her eyes had hardened.

'Really, Mike, it's hardly in character for you to start preaching on the subject of wifely duties. The other night you were suggesting you'd appreciate it if I decided to forget I was a wife for a while.'

Mike shrugged. It was true, of course. That party night he'd have been more than willing to take Gillian to bed. Funny the way Geoff had kept reiterating that he had done that very thing! He doubted the veracity of Geoff's boast. Not that he cared one way or another if Geoff had been to bed with Gillian. He was no longer interested in her.

'Perhaps your loving husband is enjoying the attentions of his 'ministering angel'!' he taunted, suddenly jealous of the amount of time Mandy spent looking after Jon. Gillian frowned.

'Don't be such a fool, Mike. Jon's not like you. Such an idea wouldn't cross his mind. Anyway, I'm hardly expected to be jealous of a girl like Mandy, am I?'

She had expected Mike to agree at once that Mandy could not exactly be considered as competition for her. His silence forced her to look at him more closely.

'Do *you* think Mandy is attractive?' she asked. 'I would hardly think she was your type, darling.'

'As a matter of fact, I do! Oh, she hasn't got your looks, Gilly. But there's something about her . . . Well, forget it, shall we?'

'No, we won't. First you suggest my husband has designs on Mandy and now you suggest she's more attractive than I am. Am I supposed to ignore that? Or are you just trying to be ridiculous to annoy me?'

'Since it's so obviously ridiculous,

why not drop the subject?'

Gillian turned on him furiously.

'You're trying to make me jealous, Mike. Well, if that's your way of livening up the afternoon, I don't think much of it. If you can't be less boring, push off home.'

'Now, now, sheathe those claws!' Mike said, teasingly. He had not the least intention of being sent away. Sooner or later Mandy would arrive, but until then he'd play it Gillian's way.

'Mike, do stop playing with that child. You look quite ridiculous lying there on the floor. Come over here and sit beside me.'

She patted the sofa invitingly.

'Darling I don't think so,' he said. 'After all, you are a very attractive woman and I'm not sure if I would behave myself properly if I sit too close to you. Besides, you forget we have a chaperon,' he teased, lifting Timmy into the air and setting him back chuckling on his knee.

The rebuff was too well covered for

Gillian to notice it. She was satisfied by Mike's flattery but still bored.

'I'm getting fed to the teeth with toys all over the place!' she said irritably. 'I can't wait for Miss Hill to get back so Mandy and the kid can move out and let me have my house to myself again.'

Now she did have Mike's attention.

'You mean, Mandy isn't staying here permanently?'

'Of course not! She's only filling the gap. She'll have to find another job in due course.'

'But I thought you said she was . . . well, a relation of Jon's.'

'So what?' Gillian retorted. 'Just because Jon's kid brother saddled her with a child is no reason why we should have it round our necks for ever more. Of course she'll have to go!'

'But where to?'

'How should I know?' Gillian replied, yawning. 'And why should *you* care, lover-boy?'

Mike decided to watch his tongue more closely.

'Well, for one thing, we're looking for a secretary in the firm. Maybe we could give her a job.'

'So that's fine and you're welcome. Just so long as she takes the kid out of here, I don't mind where she goes!'

Mike drew out a cigarette case and lit a cigarette slowly, his eyes thoughtful.

'I thought you liked her, Gillian. You were full of her praises when she arrived.'

'My dear boy, I neither like nor dislike her. Jon says she's efficient and if he says so, she must be, so what the hell does it matter if she's likeable or not? Mike, for goodness' sake, let's talk about something interesting. I'm crashingly bored.'

'Then let's talk about you!' Mike said, grinning again. He could afford to pander for a while to Gillian's vanity. She'd just imparted some very good news. Mandy would shortly become free and *he* could employ her; have her in the office where he could see her every day, for as often or as long as he wished. At that moment, to Gillian's intense annoyance, Mandy came into the room looking untidy and flustered.

'Sorry I've been so long,' she apologised, lifting Timmy into her arms. 'I've just taken Jon some tea and there's a fresh pot made in the kitchen if you'd like it, Gillian. Hullo, Mike!' she added, noticing him properly. 'Happy Christmas!'

He was suddenly glad that he had not put that bottle of perfume by the tree as he'd planned. Gillian was no fool and might have guessed the seriousness of his interest in Mandy if he'd betrayed himself so stupidly. The present to the child was one thing. Perfume to a girl was another.

'Won't you sit down for a minute? You look exhausted,' he said, going towards a chair for her. But Mandy shook her head.

'I've got to give Timmy his tea, thanks all the same. Sorry I couldn't bring yours in, Gillian. At least I've caught up with the paper-work and, by the way, Jon said to give you his love. He's feeling miles better and looks it, too.'

Gillian made no reply. Mandy took the child out of the room and Mike stood up.

'I'd better be making a move,' he said reluctantly. 'You'll want to go and see Jon, I expect, and I've got to get back and change.'

'I told you Jon has forbidden me to go near him in case I catch the bug,' Gillian said. 'So there's no need to rush off. Don't go, Mike. Come over here and talk to me.'

She stretched herself seductively on the sofa, but Mike pretended not to notice.

'I suppose I could stay for a cup of tea,' he said ingenuously. 'Didn't Mandy say she's left a pot in the kitchen?'

'*You*, drinking *tea!*' Gillian said scathingly. 'I'll get you a proper drink, darling.'

'Really, Gilly, I'd prefer tea. I'll be drinking a lot tonight. Let's go and swill the kitchen variety.'

'All right, if you insist. You know, Mike, I've a damn good mind to come to the party, after all. I mean, why not? I can't do anything for Jon and he's better, anyway. I don't see why I should call off and stay here to be bored out of my wits. You could take me, couldn't you?'

She linked her arm through his meaningfully. He could not, this time, avoid the invitation.

'I'd love to, Gilly, you know that, but I promised Patty I'd drive to Newly and pick up some friends of hers at the station. That's all of ten miles in the wrong direction. Perhaps you could get a taxi to take you? I just won't have time.'

Gillian withdrew her arm furiously.

'No, thanks. I'm not in the habit of going to parties unescorted. I'll give Geoff a ring. He can fetch me.'

'That's a good idea!' Mike said as naturally as he could. The last thing he wanted was to make an enemy of

Gillian and be barred from the house. Gillian was not one to take rejection well. She simply wasn't used to it. 'Tell you what,' he added. 'I'll ask Geoff when I get home if he'll go to Newly. Then I can come to collect you. Okay, Gilly?'

She nodded, mollified. For one moment she had thought Mike was giving her the brush-off.

'Now, how about that tea?' he reminded her.

She still looked sulky as she took him into the kitchen. Timmy was in a high-chair and, as Mike had hoped, Mandy was sitting beside him cutting up bread and butter fingers.

'Such domesticity is hardly your scene, darling, is it?' Gillian murmured, *sotto voce*.

Mike made no reply. Gillian was right, of course. Toddlers and tea in a kitchen strung with nappies airing on an old-fashioned pulley were, until this Christmas afternoon, outside his experience. Yet he was discovering he liked it. The atmosphere was friendly, cosy in the literal meaning of the word.

He sat down at the table and put one of Timmy's bread and butter fingers in his mouth. The child stared at him solemnly as if to accuse him of theft. Mike laughed and Mandy joined in.

It was the first time he had seen her laugh so openly and happily and Mike felt his excitement growing. She was even more attractive when happy than with that sad, mysterious preoccupied air which had first aroused his interest. He wished very much that Gillian were elsewhere so that he could talk to Mandy about herself. He wanted to know so much about her, her age, her relationship to the child's father and whether she had really been in love with the fellow. Somehow he doubted very much that she was the type for casual affairs. He knew the kid was Jon's nephew and wondered whether Jon would see eye to eye with Gillian about turning Mandy and the boy out of the house once she had served her purpose.

It did not seem probable. Although Jon was not really his type, Mike quite liked him — the little he'd seen of him — and he did not think Jon would turn her out.

One thing had been quite clear that evening he and Jock, Patty and Geoff had dined here and that was Jon's adoration of Gilly. His eyes had followed her everywhere and Mike had been amused and a trifle sorry for the guy, since his young wife clearly did not have the same worship for him. Mike could understand the fascination Gilly had for her husband, as for other men. She was the epitome of sheer physical attraction in a lithe, feline, tigerish way. She knew how to use her body to attract. He, himself, had imagined what it would be like making love to her, taming her, making her submit, subduing that proud, independent, self-assured arrogance; dominating the indomitable. She was a challenge to any man.

But attracted as he was, he had not

liked her, had quickly discovered how spoilt, self-centred and selfish she was as a character. If she didn't get her own way she was sulky and moody and he could well imagine that she could be vicious. There was a latent cruelty under the exterior charm which repelled even as it fascinated. She would have no hesitation in turning Mandy out if it suited her and could easily override Jon's kindlier instincts.

Whilst these thoughts were passing through his mind, he heard Gillian telling Mandy that she had made up her mind to go to the Christmas party at the Matthews' house after all. Mike noticed that expression of dismay on Mandy's face — or was it disapproval? — as she said:

'But, Gillian, I thought you'd be going up to sit with Jon. He's so much better and I know he wants . . . ' She broke off, as if she realised that it was not for her to tell Jon's wife where her duty lay.

Gillian was looking furious.

'Jon knows very well I'm no good in a sickroom. Besides, he doesn't want me to catch the 'flu and, even if he *is* better, he is still infectious. I'll put my head round the door before I go.' She gave a contrived little laugh and, turning to Mike, said: 'Mandy's terribly old-fashioned. She thinks a wife's place is at her husband's side, not trotting off to parties. She hasn't been with us long enough to know that Jon *wants* me to have a good time — in so far as it's possible in this dump!' she added bitterly.

Mike saw the colour rush into Mandy's cheeks and fade away leaving shadows under her eyes. She looked drained and unhappy.

His feelings of pity were mixed with irritation. Mandy should stand up for herself. Gillian could all too easily be a bully if Mandy allowed it, turning her into a household slave, if she wasn't already that. Gillian even left the answering of the telephone to her so that she was seldom off her feet for more than a few minutes at a time.

'I must be off,' he said, suddenly wishing himself out of the house and away from its problems and undercurrents. As Gilly had pointed out, it really wasn't his scene and he'd be a fool to let himself become too deeply involved. It wasn't his job to protect Mandy. He was behaving as if he were in love with her and that certainly did not fit in with his plans to remain a bachelor for a good few years to come.

As he left the house he congratulated himself on using a little common sense. He was well out of it. He no longer wanted an affair with Gillian and he knew instinctively that Mandy was not the type of girl who would want an affair with him. The next man she became involved with would be a potential husband and father to the kid — and that man was not Mike Sinclair!

I'll keep well away from there! he promised himself as he drove home. It was a promise he was to find impossible to keep.

Mandy carried the supper tray into Jon's room and forced a bright smile as she propped the pillows up behind him.

'Turkey soup and a baked custard!' she announced. 'You specified a very light supper, Doctor, so I've not included Christmas pudding and mince pies.'

Jon returned the smile.

'I couldn't have eaten them. Thanks, Mandy. I feel an awful fraud lying in bed letting you wait on me. I'm so much better, I'm sure I could get up.'

'That's ridiculous. Dr Harvey said you were to stay in bed for at least forty-eight hours after your temperature had gone down and you still have a temperature. Now I'm beginning to understand why people say doctors make terrible patients.'

He grinned ruefully.

'I'll try not to complain, Nurse!' His face became serious as he looked at her and said: 'I'm not sure that you shouldn't be the patient, Mandy. You're doing too much. Is Gilly giving you a hand? You look exhausted.'

'Yes, of course she is,' Mandy lied. Gillian had done nothing but cook the lunch. She wondered if she should gently break the news to Jon that his wife was off to yet another party tonight. She sensed he would be hurt and dreaded the look that would come into his face. She decided to let Gillian do her own dirty work. 'Do stop worrying, Jon. Everything's fine and even your patients have decided to co-operate and not be ill on Christmas Day.'

'The Fergusson baby not arrived yet?'

'No. Dr Harvey saw Mrs Fergusson yesterday, but it was a false alarm. Now eat up before it all gets cold.'

'Then, while I'm eating, sit down and talk to me. While we're on the subject, tell me about Timmy's birth. I always meant to ask you about it. Obviously you didn't have him at the home.'

'No, in hospital,' Mandy said, sitting down as he had asked in order to make him eat. 'It wasn't too bad, I suppose. Everyone tried to be kind. I was called 'Mrs' in the ward, but the nurses and the other patients knew I wasn't married. You see, there was no proud father coming to sit with me after the baby was born.'

A look of dismay crossed Jon's face.

'That's awful!' he said quietly. 'If I'd known . . . '

'It wasn't too bad!' Mandy broke in untruthfully. 'It was much worse for the girls who weren't keeping their babies. I had Timmy and I knew I was going to keep him. It was awful for the girls who had decided on adoption. Some of them even refused to see their babies, so they had nothing at all — no one to make the pain and discomfort worth while. I was lucky.'

'And brave!' Jon said. 'Tell me, Mandy, did you honestly realise then how difficult it would be bringing Timmy up on your own?'

'I don't know. I think so. Everyone tried to warn me how difficult it would be. I don't think it would have made any difference if I'd had a preview of what was to come. I just knew I couldn't part with him, especially after he was born.'

'You must be glad now,' Jon agreed warmly. 'He's a lovely child and you've brought him up beautifully.'

Mandy sighed.

'So far, perhaps. But I worry about the future, especially with him being a boy. Boys need a father when they get older. I won't be enough for him then.'

Jon nodded.

'But by the time he's old enough to want a man around the place, you'll have married, Mandy. I just hope, whoever he is, he'll be worthy of you and Timmy. I think I shall insist on being allowed to vet any likely candidates. After all, I am Timmy's uncle, even if I'm not legally your brother-in-law.'

Mandy was silent. She could not tell

Jon that her prospects of getting married were even less probable than before she had met *him*. She believed that love was essential for a happy marriage and she was incapable of loving any man now. If Jon had been free . . . and by some miracle were to fall in love with her . . . But those were thoughts she dared not consider because they were too frightening. She did not *want* to love him. She wanted, above all, to stay in the safe cage of immunity she had so carefully erected round herself when Pete died. She'd been happy enough, concentrating her emotions on Timmy and her energies on the simple act of survival. Falling in love with Jon was a disaster she had never anticipated, never for one moment imagined, when she agreed to come and live in his house. For two days now she had been fighting the truth, telling herself over and over again that it was only Jon's resemblance to Pete which made her imagine she was in love with him. But the truth kept surfacing at unexpected moments, refusing to be denied. As she sat beside his bed, she found herself dreading the thought that in a few minutes the happy, contented expression on his face would give way to hurt and depression at the knowledge that Gillian couldn't care less about him. Her behaviour since Jon had gone down with 'flu was inexplicable to Mandy, even though Gillian had explained her phobia about illness. Even making allowances for it, there was no excusing her total lack of concern for Jon's health except in so far as it affected her social programme over Christmas! She had not once asked Mandy if Jon's temperature were up or down; nor enquired except in the most perfunctory way at breakfast what kind of night he had had, whether or not the doctor was calling to see him again. Even if she, Gillian, were truly afraid of catching a germ, she could still have sent Jon messages of affection and concern via Mandy, or written him little notes, or even called through the doorway. And now, as if to add insult to injury, she was going off to a party — on Christmas Day. How could Jon fail to feel hurt and neglected!

Although she knew she had no right to interfere, Mandy longed to make Gillian's behaviour seem less callous to Jon. Impulsively she said:

'Mike Sinclair was here to tea. He talked Gillian into going to the Matthews' party tonight. I don't think she really wanted to go without you, Jon, but Mike made her feel she would be letting everyone down if she stayed home. I know she doesn't really want to leave you.'

Jon did not look up. He gave no sign that he was surprised or annoyed or upset. When he did speak it was to say quite casually:

'Of course Gilly must go. When you see her, Mandy, tell her I quite understand and she's not to give it another thought.' He looked up then and said thoughtfully: 'I just wish you could go, too, Mandy. How long since you went to a party? A long while, I imagine!'

'I suppose it is,' Mandy agreed. 'But don't feel sorry about it, Jon. I'll be glad to drop into bed and sleep. A party is the very last thing I feel like tonight.'

'You've been absolutely wonderful, Mandy. As soon as I'm on my feet again, I'm going to make it up to you. We'll find a baby-sitter for Timmy and get Mike or Geoff or someone as a fourth and we'll have a party you'll remember for a long while. That's a promise! In fact, forthcoming babies permitting, and assuming I've got rid of this damned 'flu, we'll make it New Year's Eve. You'd like that, wouldn't you? I think Gilly has a table booked at the Country Club — never can remember its name — for their New Year's Eve dinner-dance. Would you like to go there?'

'It sounds fabulous — if I had anything to wear!'

Jon gave a smug little smile.

'And that settles something else I've

had on my mind — what to give you for Christmas. You're to buy yourself a new dress, Mandy, and give me the bill. And don't start arguing about it. It'll give me great pleasure. It hasn't been much of a Christmas for you, one way and another, and it'll give me a chance to make up for it. Agreed, Mandy? Say yes, if only to please me.'

She nodded. To be wearing a new dress and go dancing with Jon — how could she refuse? At the back of her mind, she knew it would be a mistake. To be with Jon on New Year's Eve, dance with him, maybe have him kiss her at midnight when the bells rang in the New Year would only be fuel to the smouldering fire of newly awakened love. Jon was Gillian's husband and she had no right even to think of loving him in the most secret part of her mind. If she chose a new dress, it would be chosen because she felt he would like it; when she wore it, it would be in the hope that he would admire her in it; when he danced with her, she would be thinking only of what it felt like to be in his arms. And if he kissed her . . .

'A penny for them, Mandy. You look miles away.'

He watched the colour flare into her cheeks and felt suddenly embarrassed, as if he had sought to intrude on some very intimate personal side of her life. Quickly he continued talking as if the question had not been asked. 'Tell me what you think of Mike Sinclair. I gather I owe him a vote of thanks for helping get me to bed when I collapsed. I've not really thanked you either, Mandy. It must have given you quite a fright.'

'I think I was more frightened that you were delirious,' Mandy said, glad to have the conversation impersonal again. 'Dr Harvey was reassuring, though. He explained there were lots of people who reacted like that with a high temperature. I'll know next time!'

They smiled at each other. Jon thought:

I've been terribly lucky to get hold of

her. When Gilly suggested we get her to replace Miss Hill, I didn't think much of the idea. As it has turned out, Mandy's lack of experience on the medical side has been far outweighed by her common sense and efficiency. In many ways she's worth a dozen Miss Hills.

After she had left the room with his supper tray he toyed with the idea of keeping Mandy on permanently. If he could somehow get rid of Miss Hill, he'd really like to keep Mandy with them. Not just because he'd grown to love little Timmy, but because every day he was appreciating Mandy more and more. He reckoned that Pete would have been a very lucky guy if he'd lived and married her. She'd have made a wonderful wife. Somehow he, Jon, and Gilly must try to find her a good husband. He'd talk to Gilly about it as soon as he was up and about again.

His thoughts switched to his wife and he frowned. He doubted the truth of Mandy's story. It would hardly need

Mike to talk Gillian into going to the Matthews' party! Gillian never refused an invitation that got her out of the house and into company. She craved people, social contact, the stimulus that a crowd seemed to give her. It was a side of her nature he couldn't reciprocate. Loving her as he did, he wanted her all to himself; he had no desire to share her with a noisy bunch of strangers. He saw this possessiveness as a fault in himself; tried whenever possible to overcome it; just as he was trying now not to be hurt that his wife should prefer to go out on Christmas Day than remain at home with him. He reasoned that since she would not be sitting with him anyway, it was pointless for her to cancel the party. But no matter how hard he tried to justify Gillian's desertion a feeling of depression engulfed him. He longed to see his bedroom door open and for Gilly to come in, looking, as always, stunningly beautiful; for her to come over and sit where Mandy had sat; to hold his hand

and tell him to hurry up and get better because she missed seeing him around the place; and most of all he wanted to hear her say she was lonely by herself in the spare room and wanted to come back here with him; to lie beside him, hold him in her arms, love him . . .

When Gillian opened the bedroom door he feigned sleep. Taken in by his closed eyes and steady breathing, her face relaxed with relief that she need not see the look of silent reproach in his eyes. She made no attempt to wake him and closed the door softly before going quietly down the stairs.

8

For the four days following Christmas, Mike was seldom out of the house. Either he stopped by in the morning to give Mandy and Timmy a lift to the day nursery, or else he was there in his car to collect them both at teatime. Usually he stayed to tea, ostensibly to see Gillian, who, he suspected uneasily, was as infatuated with him as he was with Mandy.

The situation might have amused him had he not felt so serious about his feelings for Mandy. As it was, Gillian's possessiveness was becoming a bore, to say the least, she was alternatively angry or seductive, depending upon whether he was focusing his attention on her or not.

Jon was now downstairs convalescing and since Gillian was forced to use some restraint in front of her husband,

Mike was able on these occasions to concentrate on Mandy. As far as he could tell, Mandy seemed to like him well enough and was always touchingly grateful when he gave her a lift or ran some errand for her. Superficially, they were now good friends but he was impatient to go a stage further and desperately anxious to know what *she* felt about *him*. He never had a chance to speak to her alone for long. Sooner rather than later Gillian would interrupt any conversation he had begun with Mandy and Mandy would make some excuse and remove herself elsewhere.

Gillian was taking very little trouble to hide her feelings. She was bitterly jealous. When she had Mike alone she said quite openly:

'You're always hanging around that girl, Mike. Anyone would think you were attracted! You're making an absolute fool of yourself.'

It was on the tip of Mike's tongue to tell Gilly once and for all that he was fast falling in love with Mandy. But a sixth sense warned him to keep his mouth shut. Gillian would make a deadly enemy and he wasn't sure enough of his welcome in this house by Mandy to risk antagonising Gillian.

'I doubt your husband would like it if I spent every moment I was here chatting you up!' he said lightly. 'Or do you want to make him jealous?'

'Has he cause to be jealous?' Gillian retorted, only half mollified. 'Seems to me you're keeping all the charm for Mandy. We had something going for us, Mike. I wasn't imagining it, was I? I'm beginning to think you don't even like me these days!'

With some difficulty he shrugged this off as nonsense. Gillian eyed him speculatively. She did not care for this feeling of uncertainty. Before Christmas she'd been reasonably certain she could have Mike for a lover any time she chose. Now she wasn't so sure. He was always hanging round the house, of course, but that was as far as it went.

Putting it quite bluntly to herself, he had stopped flirting with her. But that wasn't quite the case, either. He still flirted with her, but in such a way that he used the extravagant compliments, the 'darlings' and the exaggerated hugs and kisses as a kind of barrier, making a parody of any real feeling between them.

'How's my gorgeous Gilly?' he'd say, his arms round her and his lips touching both cheeks like a French general. It was a lot of nonsense to which even Jon took no exception and merely laughed, saying: 'Now then, Mike, you should be asking me how *my* gorgeous Gilly is. Kindly remember that it's my wife you're kissing!' To which Mike would grin and pay her some further compliment, such as: 'I just can't keep my hands off her, Jon. She's irresistible.'

He never touched or kissed Mandy. That much was some consolation to Gillian, for it did not cross her mind that Mike could be seriously attracted to Mandy as long as she, Gillian, was available.

Gillian did not altogether understand her own conflicting emotions. Mike had become a serious challenge — someone she wanted to fall adoringly at her feet the way all men she desired always ended up when she set out to attract them. She told herself that Mike had been around women long enough to guess that his playing hard-to-get would arouse her much more quickly than the easy conquest. She had to admit it was working, too. She was now determined to have him for a lover. Consideration for Jon simply didn't enter into what had now become a battle of wills between herself and Mike. So far Mike was winning.

She consoled herself with the thought of the New Year's Eve dinner-dance. There were now eight people involved, Jon, herself, Mike, Mandy, Patty, Jock, Geoff and another girl called Sue. She planned to appropriate Mike, to slip out of the dance with him to the car park and let him seduce her if he wished. She'd see that he did wish, too! She had bought a new dress with a deep plunging neckline, made of clinging satin that would outline all the perfect curves of her body. With champagne flowing, Mike would succumb quickly enough, she was certain. She had only to bide her time.

Mike, too, was eagerly awaiting the party. He, too, had plans. He intended to make Mandy his partner and appropriate her for the evening. He was prepared for Gilly to fume and rage. He wouldn't care once he'd woken Mandy's interest in him. Gillian couldn't stop him dating Mandy if she wanted to go out with him.

He found himself suddenly sympathetic towards Jon. It must be hell, he decided, to be so much in love with your wife and have to see her making up to other guys. Or didn't Jon realise what a little tramp he'd married? Because Gillian looked so flawless, did Jon believe she was beyond corruption, or incapable of corrupting! Was he too blinded by her beauty to see the truth?

It was Mike's private opinion that if Jon wanted to keep Gillian for himself he'd better start putting his foot down and stop giving her the opportunity to be unfaithful. Jon was too nice to Gillian, too kind and easy-going. Morever, he still looked far from well.

Jon was by no means feeling a hundred per cent. Fortunately, Dr Harvey was still coping with the work and promised to stay till after the New Year. Jon was determined to be fit enough for the party. He'd spoilt enough fun for Gilly over Christmas, and New Year's Eve was special for them, being the anniversary of the first time they'd met. He was sure Gilly remembered for several times she'd told him that she'd die of disappointment if he weren't well enough to go and the party had to be called off.

She had not yet returned to their bedroom, still afraid of the 'flu germs lurking round, she had said, although he and Dr Harvey had assured her there was no further risk of infection. He hated being parted from her at night and fully intended to remedy that situation after the New Year dance. It was for Mandy's sake, too, that the party must take place. She'd bought herself a dress on his insistence and had shown it to him as it lay in its box, as radiant as a child with a longed-for toy. He'd been touched by her pleasure in it as much as by her anxiety that it might have cost too much.

'It seems awful to have spent so much on a dress I may not wear again for ages and ages!' she said guiltily.

Jon had laughed.

'Nonsense. You forget I'm used to Gilly's extravagant purchases. It sounds very cheap to me. As to you not wearing it again for 'ages and ages',' he'd mimicked her voice, making her smile, 'I seem to have noticed a certain young man around this house at not infrequent intervals of late. I fancy Mike has no intention of leaving you to hide in obscurity.'

'That's ridiculous!' Mandy had flared up with unusual indignation. 'Mike doesn't come to see me, he comes to see . . . ' She broke off, flushing red with embarrassment, but Jon only laughed.

'To see Gilly? That's just a cover, Mandy. You're the one he looks at when he thinks no one is noticing him. I know the symptoms only too well from personal experience. When you're in love — in the beginning, that is — you're afraid of a rebuff or that someone will notice, so you go out of your way to avoid the one person you want to be with. One puts on a great show of indifference which is, in itself, a give-away to anyone looking for signs. All that carry-on with Gilly is Mike's way of covering up what he feels for you.'

Mandy seemed prepared to believe it. She had pretended to do so lest Jon should realise that Gilly was serious enough about Mike even if he were not serious about her. Her woman's instinct gave her a clearer picture of Gillian's true feelings than Jon seemed to have. But then Gilly's behaviour with Mike was more revealing when Jon was not there. Despite Mandy's presence, Gillian was openly seductive in a way Mandy found quite intolerable, knowing how much Jon loved her. She could not bear the thought of his hurt if he knew. Her dislike of Gillian had by now turned to a burning hatred. It was beyond her to understand how Jon could be so blind to Gillian's true character. She fought hard to ignore such thoughts, telling herself they were based on jealousy and that Gillian probably loved Jon very much in her own way.

Her own growing love for Jon frightened her by its intensity and by its terrible insistence on being recognised. Determined though she was to bury it in her subconscious, never to give it a chance to root, Jon was constantly there in her mind, gentle, patient, grateful, generous and always thoughtful for her welfare. He was wonderful with Timmy, too, playing with the little boy for hours on end, finding ways to amuse and interest him. It was hard not to see Jon as the perfect father. Timmy adored him. But then he loved Mike, too, who was almost as good with him as Jon. The only trouble with Mike was that he tended to over-excite Timmy and since he was so often there to tea, it usually meant a chaotic bedtime!

Mandy smiled at the thought of Mike piggy-backing Timmy up the stairs for his bath. Mike had been like a kid himself, fooling around with boats in the water, splashing himself and the floor as he entered whole-heartedly into the game he'd invented on Timmy's behalf. It was impossible not to like Mike. Perhaps, if it were not for Jon, she might even have fallen a little in love with him. He had Pete's impulsive, irrational and somewhat irresponsible make-up, the very opposite of her own. But apart from Timmy they had little in common, any more than she and Pete had shared interests. She knew now that marriage to Pete would have been a disaster because she now found her mind, her thoughts, her whole approach, so simply and perfectly in tune with Jon's. With Pete she realised it had been the attraction of the opposite and that was all. His mind had never been in tune with hers as Jon's was, invariably.

As she dressed in preparation for the New Year dinner-dance, Mandy tried very hard to convince herself that it was for Mike's benefit she was making herself attractive, that it was his compliments she was eagerly anticipating, his arms she wanted around her when she danced, that it would be Mike standing next to her when the New Year was rung in and his lips, not Jon's, that she wanted to feel on hers at that moment.

The one thing she dreaded beyond all others was that Jon should discover how she felt. She swore to herself that no one would ever know and she, herself, would begin the New Year by never thinking of it.

The evening started badly. Jon and Gillian were as close to a row as Mandy had ever seen. Gillian looked outrageously beautiful in the most revealing gown she could have chosen to wear. Jon felt that whilst it might pass in London, it was a bit too revealing for their locality, more especially as Gillian was the wife of the local doctor.

They were still discussing the matter heatedly when Mandy walked into the drawing room. Gillian looked furious as she explained Jon's objections to Mandy. Jon looked upset.

'I think the dress is beautiful and Gilly looks beautiful in it,' he said, appealing to Mandy. 'It's just that there may well be one of two of my older patients there who'll find it slightly outrageous. They're a stuffy, old-fashioned lot, but I can't afford to offend them, especially as the older generation are mostly private patients, who, I might say, have a vast influence in the town.'

Gillian's face was thunderous.

'If you think I'm going to start wearing dreary, ugly, dated, provincial clothes, just because you're afraid to upset your stupid old patients, you've got another think coming, Jon. You said you liked the dress and so do I, so what the hell!'

Jon, unexpectedly formal in a dinner jacket, went to the side table and poured himself a whisky. He looked very pale but determined.

'I'm sorry, darling, but you've got to go along with me on this. I'm only asking you to make the dress . . . well, a little less revealing. If you could stitch it up the front just a bit?'

'I won't. It's the fashion and, anyway, what's wrong with my breasts? Other men seem to find them attractive, even if you don't!'

'That's unfair. You're deliberately refusing to see my point of view. If you . . .'

'Oh, for God's sake!' Gillian interrupted violently. 'I thought you were a bit more broadminded, Jon. It's bad enough living in this boring little town without you wanting me to bring myself down to that level. Well, I'm not a provincial and I never will be one and I'll wear what I please. And don't run off, Mandy. Come here so Jon can look you over.' She turned to Jon, her eyes blazing. 'I suppose you'd rather I wore a respectable little outfit like Mandy's, would you? Well, I wouldn't be seen dead in it.'

'Gillian!' Jon's voice was sharp with anger. He stepped forward, looking for one moment as if he might strike her. Mandy quickly intervened.

'Jon, she didn't mean it that way. Please!'

Jon looked down at the small heart-shaped face and with difficulty mastered his temper. He and Gillian had no right to involve Mandy in the argument, ruin the evening she'd been looking forward to so much. Gilly's cruelty about her dress was bad enough.

'I think you look beautiful,' he said gently. 'And what's more, I mean it. The outfit is neither dreary nor provincial. It's lovely.'

Mandy felt like weeping as she stood there, Jon's hands on her bare forearms, her whole body tense as she waited for a fresh outburst from Gillian. Instead Gillian said calmly:

'I'm sorry, Mandy. In fact the dress is okay and just right on you. Those off-beat browns and mauves show up your fair hair and you look . . . well, prettier than I've ever seen you.'

Too surprised to speak, Mandy stood silently as Jon released his hold on her and went across to Gillian.

'That was nice of you, darling,' he said, all anger gone from his voice. 'And I'm sorry if I upset you about your dress. If you want to wear it, then to hell with my patients. I'll be more than proud of you.'

Mandy caught her breath. Gillian

was clever, far cleverer than she had ever imagined. She knew Jon, knew how to play on his love to get her own way. It was a subtle move and somehow deadly, for it proved she had no real thought for Jon's wishes, for his feelings. She had known Jon would weaken if she changed her tone.

Jon hustled them out to the car, and Mandy felt like turning back and rushing up to her room. She no longer wanted to go to the party, her depression deepening with every moment that passed. It was not for herself she felt so depressed, but for Jon. Gillian should have foreseen that such a dress, beautiful though it was, would be far too extreme for the occasion. Quite probably she had forseen it and simply didn't care. Whatever her reasoning, she had ruined Jon's evening and she must know it.

Matters were not improved when they met Mike who was waiting for them in the club foyer. He took one look at Gillian and whistled.

'Wow! That'll turn a few heads, Gilly!' he said without realising how tactless his remark was.

Mandy stepped forward quickly before Jon could speak and in a false, bright little voice, wished Mike a Happy New Year.

Mike looked down at her, surprised to find her so unusually forthcoming.

'And a Happy New Year to you, too, Beautiful!' he said. 'Can I take your coat?'

Mandy was glad that they had Mike, with his slick, easy chatter, to walk with them through the crowded foyer to the equally crowded lounge where the rest of the party was waiting for them. She was aware, and knew that Jon was, too, of all the heads turning as Gillian walked by. She noticed the expression on Geoff's face and the wink he gave Patty's husband, Jock, as if to say: Look what we've got for the evening!

Gillian seated herself calmly between Mike and Geoff and Mandy was given the empty chair beside Jon. Mike ordered drinks and conversation began to flow. Jon's eyes were fastened on Gillian, his expression enigmatic as he watched her raise her glass to Mike, her long lashes only half lifted as she smiled at him, saying: 'Happy New Year, lover-boy!'

'I think she's the most beautiful woman in the room!' Mandy said impulsively, hating Gillian yet admiring her at the same time.

Jon looked at her quizzically.

'You really mean that, don't you? If Gilly's the most beautiful, you're the most generous. Another woman might not have forgiven her so readily.'

'But for Gillian I wouldn't be here!' Mandy replied. 'I owe her my job with you, don't I? But for her I'd probably be seeing the New Year in all by myself at Mrs Phillips' boarding house.'

'Then I'm happy you're happy,' Jon said warmly. 'And we'll make this the happiest night of your life. Whatever you want shall be yours, Cinderella.

Now who will you choose for your Prince Charming? Mike, I think, in preference to Brother Geoff?'

Because he was brightening up, Mandy played the game with him.

'Yes, definitely Mike. He looks rather good in a dinner jacket. He's very nice-looking.'

'Then I personally shall ensure you sit next to him at dinner,' Jon promised. 'From then on it's up to you to ravish the young man with your intelligent conversation and your womanly charms. I don't, somehow, think that will be difficult. You may not have noticed in your modest little way that he keeps staring at you. You really do look very attractive, Mandy.'

Happiness welled through her. She knew she ought not to let Jon's compliments affect her in this way, but she could not wish them unsaid.

The head waiter brought menus and was, like every other man in the room, unable to keep his eyes off Gillian. Jon, noticing, was pretending not to do so and Gillian, with some devil of mischief in her, was flaunting her naked shoulders, breasts and neck with an amused smile on her face. It was as if she had set out deliberately to antagonise Jon, showing him by her behaviour that she did not give two hoots for any of his patients who might be disapproving. And Jon was refusing to be drawn.

It was a relief to Mandy when they finally went into dinner and Jon, true to his promise, seated her next to Mike.

'This is nice!' Mike said warmly as he held her chair for her. 'Now I have you beside me I'm really getting into the party spirit!'

She smiled back at him. It was very easy to be light-hearted and chat back to Mike. She sensed his interest in her and was flattered that he could find time for her with Gillian at the same table. She did not understand why he should find her attractive, but the mood was not one for self-analysis or seriousness. She let herself relax and flirted back. Halfway through the meal

Mike said softly:

'You're a different girl tonight, Mandy. I'd begun to think you always took life seriously. Tonight you're being your age.'

'Sorry to disappoint you!' Mandy replied cheerfully. The third glass of champagne had now gone to her head. She told him so, adding: 'If I get silly, tell me. I don't want to disgrace myself!'

'You're certainly not doing that!' Mike answered. 'You're good company, Mandy, as well as adorably pretty. You're going to dance with me later, I hope? I want every dance with you.'

'I don't know if I'll be able to stand up. I'll try!'

'I'll hold you. I can't wait to do just that. Did you know I was falling in love with you?'

It was said in the same light-hearted tone, but the look in his eyes was probing, disturbing. Quickly Mandy said:

'Then you'd better stop, Mike,

because I haven't the slightest intention of falling in love with anyone. I should hate to make you unhappy on New Year's Eve.'

'Ah, but I shan't be unhappy. You don't think I'd take your very first 'No' seriously, do you? I shall set myself to undermine all your intentions to remain locked away from the cruel world. I'm going to bring you back to life, Mandy. How does that sound?'

'What makes you think I'm withdrawn from life?' Mandy retorted. 'On the contrary, I'm very much involved.'

'Who with?' Mike shot back at her, the question coming too quickly and unexpectedly for her to prepare herself.

'No one!' she said firmly. But the hot colour was rising slowly to her cheeks and she knew that Mike had noticed. She was furious with him, but most of all with herself for blushing like some silly schoolgirl.

'I *want* to believe you!' Mike was saying, his eyes no longer teasing. 'Gilly told me you didn't have a current boyfriend, so I don't see who my rival could be.'

'I told you there was no one!' Mandy was almost shouting and sensed Geoff on her left-hand side, turning away from Gillian to glance at her. 'This is silly, Mike,' she said quietly and evenly. 'I've told you there is no one and that's the end of it.'

''Methinks thou dost protest too much!'' Mike quoted. 'However, I'll take your word for it because I want to believe it. From now on, I'm claiming you for my girl. How about it?'

Mandy was saved a reply by the arrival of the waiter with the next course. Mike's turn of conversation had thoroughly disturbed her; not because she objected to his overtures, which she did not take seriously, but because she had so nearly betrayed herself. Even now she was finding it an effort not to keep glancing up at the top of the table to see what Jon was doing; to whom he was talking; if he was still worried about Gillian's dress or her behaviour. If only she could convince herself that she was not in love with Jon! No one knew better than she did how hopelessly wrong it was for her to love him. He belonged to Gillian and he loved his wife no matter how badly she behaved. If only Gillian returned his love and she could believe Jon was happy! But whenever she did glance his way, and he thought no one was looking at him, his face was that of a man being tortured. He looked strained, taut, ill and utterly miserable. When anyone spoke to him the mask was put back at once and no one would have thought him other than a man in the best of spirits, enjoying a gala dinner with his wife and friends.

Mandy was unaware when she stole those glances at Jon that Mike in his turn was watching her. He was shaken deeply as the truth slowly dawned on him that Mandy loved Jon! For the first time in his life, Mike was jealous. He found himself remembering that Jon was the brother of the boy who'd made

Mandy his mistress and given her a child. Was Jon like him? Was it just because of the resemblance that Mandy was attracted to him? A hundred questions demanded answers, but he knew this was no time to reveal his knowledge to Mandy. He could not even be sure if he had imagined that look of love on her face. He preferred to believe that having nursed Jon through the 'flu recently, those looks were merely of concern for his health. But if it were true . . .

Mike's thoughts switched. Nothing could come of it even if he were right and Mandy was in love with Jon. Jon had eyes only for Gillian. If ever a man was in love with his wife, it was he.

So I still have a chance! he told himself, feeling happy again. Mandy must know it's hopeless. A happily married man has nothing to offer her. But I, thank God, am not married.

Mike would have been happier still if he had known that Mandy's thoughts were now running along exactly the same lines. Mike was free. He was fun. And he found her attractive. She would do better, she told herself severely, to concentrate all her thoughts on Mike and forget Jon in so far as it was possible. Mike could help her to forget.

So she allowed herself to be monopolised for the rest of the evening. She made no objection when he held her tightly against him on the dance floor and every time her eyes closed, and she found herself imagining she was in Jon's arms, she fought against it. When Mike kissed her fingers and then her palm at the end of each dance she did not draw her hand away but let him continue to hold it.

Halfway through the evening, when they returned to their table, thirsty, needing a drink and brief rest, Gillian leant across the table, ignoring Mandy as she said icily to Mike:

'Isn't it time you remembered your manners and had a dance with me?'

Mike laughed, but Gillian's eyes were blazing with anger and when he stood up at once to dance with her, she said furiously:

'No, thanks. This one's half over. I'll have a whole dance if you can spare the time, Mike.'

She gave Mandy a look of pure hatred. Mandy bit her lip in her embarrassment. It was impossible for anyone at the table not to know that Gillian was seething with jealousy, that she wanted Mike for herself. She dared not look across the table at Jon and see the same awareness in his face. But as the dance came to an end and a fresh one started, even before Mike could speak, she heard Jon say:

'Don't go to sleep, Mandy. I'd like this dance with you.'

She knew she was trembling as she walked on to the floor beside him. As his arm went round her, she shivered uncontrollably. Jon said:

'I'm afraid Gilly upset you. You mustn't let her, Mandy. She doesn't mean to be unkind. It's just that she's been used all her life to having undivided attention from all around. Mike's appropriation of you hurt her pride. In a way, you should be complimented.'

'Don't *you* mind?' The words were out before she could prevent them. She heard him catch his breath before he answered quietly:

'I'm human enough to feel jealous at times until I remember I'm married to a woman who has been beautiful all her life and therefore expects and needs homage paid to that beauty. She doesn't mean to hurt me any more than she means to hurt you.'

Mandy felt near to weeping. He was hurt, whatever face he might put on it. Jealous, too, as he had every right to be. When Mike and Gillian danced past them, Gillian had her hand at the nape of Mike's neck and her beautiful body was pressed against his. She no longer looked angry, but soft and desirable and desiring, too. Then Mike caught Mandy's eye and winked and she felt herself relaxing and she laughed. No matter how romantic Gillian was feeling, Mike wasn't taking it seriously.

His mind running along the same lines, Jon said:

'Your Prince Charming is very attentive to you, Cinderella. I hope the ball is to your satisfaction?'

'It's wonderful!' Mandy said. 'You know, I haven't had a party like this since . . . since Pete was alive. I really do feel like Cinderella. It was so good of you to arrange it all. I'm very grateful.'

Jon's arm tightened around her.

'It's lovely to be able to do things for you, Mandy. You're so appreciative. In fact, you're a very sweet girl.'

Mandy felt her heart melting. She closed her eyes and felt Jon's cheek against her hair. The moment was unbearably poignant and she gave way to it, allowing her body to relax and move in perfect rhythm with Jon's. He danced beautifully and she had no difficulty in following him to the slow dreamy music the group was now playing.

She felt his hand tighten over hers and her heart lurched, her whole being aching now with longing. She had forgotten what it was like to love and be loved and now, in this isolated moment in time, she was alive in every part of her being.

Afraid of the intensity of her feelings, she tried to draw away, but he said: 'No, stay close, Mandy. You dance beautifully.'

He had no idea of hurting her; no idea of her feelings for him, or even any conscious knowledge of his feelings for her. He knew only that he had been tired and dispirited and desperately lonely and now, suddenly, he was holding warmth and sweetness and tenderness in his arms. Mandy was so slim and supple, her body moulding perfectly to his, her perfume so unlike Gillian's heady, pungent scent, a tantalising whisper of golden days and fresh spring mornings.

'It's a lovely perfume you're wearing,'

he said dreamily. 'What's it called, Mandy?'

'It's Estée Lauder's Youth Dew — frantically expensive!' she told him happily. 'Mike gave it to me on Boxing Day as a belated Christmas present. I shouldn't have accepted it, I suppose, but I liked it so much, I was tempted.'

'It's perfect for you. I wish I'd given it to you. Mandy, I owe you so much. You looked after me wonderfully. Tell me what you want most of all in the world. I'd like to give it to you, whatever it is.'

With difficulty Mandy held back the tears that had sprung so suddenly and unexpectedly to her eyes.

'You couldn't buy what I want!' she said truthfully.

Misunderstanding her, Jon said:

'One day, when I win the football pools and I'm as rich as Gulbenkian, I'll ask you again and then I will be able to afford it, whatever it is.'

Mandy was saved any further questioning by a sudden roll of drums and the announcement that it was one minute to midnight. The dancers were joined on the floor by people who had been sitting at their tables and jostled one another as friends searched for friends. Still holding her hand, Jon started off in search of Gillian, his eyes eagerly scanning the faces for that of his wife. The drums grew louder and gave way to the sound of bells and Big Ben chiming.

'It's no use!' Jon said, coming to an abrupt halt. 'I can't see any of the others.'

She sensed his disappointment and, when he turned at the stroke of midnight to look down at her, her face was a mask of sadness. Forgetting himself, aware only that no one should be unhappy at such a moment, Jon put his hand beneath her chin and raised her face to his.

'I want you to be happy,' he said. 'Happy New Year, Mandy!' And he bent his head and kissed her.

Mandy was too caught up by her

uncontrollable emotions to be aware of his. The kiss, which began in Jon's mind as pity, changed as it lingered between their lips, slowly catching fire. As the music of 'Auld Lang Syne' burst around them from a hundred voices, Jon's mouth came hard down on hers and he forgot Gillian, forgot who he was or where he was as Mandy's sweetness filled him.

'Hey! Break it up, you two!' It was Mike's voice penetrating through their oblivion, bringing them back to reality. Jon released her abruptly and smiled shakily.

'Happy New Year, Mike!' he said. Then he turned on his heel and disappeared into the crowd.

Mike looked down at Mandy's flushed face and no longer doubted his earlier suspicions. He was certain now that she was in love with Jon.

'That's enough of that!' he said jocularly, trying to ease the moment for her and at the same time to overcome the jealousy that raged through him.

'You're my girl, Mandy, and time you remembered it. Happy New Year, darling!'

He kissed her hard, meaningfully, feeling her resistance and determined to overcome it. He released her only when he tasted the salt of her tears on his lips.

'Darling Mandy, don't!' he said gently.

He put an arm around her and, allowing her to hide her face against his shoulder, guided her out of the room, out of the building, into the frosty night air towards his car.

9

Mike wrapped the car rug round her and, still holding her in his arms, let her cry. She did so silently and hopelessly. He lent her a handkerchief and when her weeping turned to an occasional sniff he said gently:

'I tried like hell to find you before midnight, but there wasn't time. Gillian was hanging on like a leech and I couldn't see you anywhere. I should have kissed you before he did, Mandy.'

She nodded.

'I know you're in love with Jon,' Mike went on tonelessly. 'It's hell for you and, believe it or not, hell for me, too. When I saw the two of you together I knew for sure what I've been fighting against all week. I love you, Mandy. I don't suppose it matters a damn to you, but, for what it's worth, I love you.'

He looked down at her tear-streaked

face and smiled.

'You don't look very pretty right now. Your mascara has run. But you're still the only girl I want, Mandy.'

She made a feeble attempt to wipe her eyes, but Mike took her hand and held it.

'Leave it. It honestly doesn't matter. You should know how little beauty matters, Mandy. Look at Gillian! If ever there was a walking example of 'all that glitters is not gold'! I can understand a man going crazy about her body, but marry her? *Why* did Jon do it?'

'He loves her!' Mandy spoke for the first time.

Mike nodded.

'I suppose he must do, or thinks he does. The fact is, he did marry her and somehow I don't think he's the kind of chap to change his mind. He's no good to you, darling.'

He pressed Mandy's hand and smiled at her wryly.

'Don't tell me to mind my own business, because you are my business whether you want to be or not. You don't really believe he would ever divorce her, do you?'

'Of course not!' Mandy said in a small choked voice. 'I never thought about it, nor would I. It's hopeless and I know it and I never meant to fall in love with him. I never meant anyone to know. I didn't even admit it to myself!'

'But when he kissed you, you had to,' Mike stated. 'So now what, Mandy? Are you going to be able to go on living there in the same house, pretending nothing has happened? Pretending you don't care?'

Mandy pulled her hand away and covered her face.

'I've got to — somehow,' she said. 'I couldn't bear it if he knew.'

'Then don't stay there. Marry me instead.'

She smiled, not taking him seriously.

'But I mean it, Mandy. I know you don't love me right now, but you'll get over Jon and I'll take the chance. I'll give you and Timmy a home, support you, take care of you. I mean it, Mandy. Marry me before you get any deeper involved.'

She stared at him disbelievingly.

'You *can't* mean it. I couldn't possibly, Mike.'

'Now don't trot out all the usual trite remarks about 'it wouldn't be fair to you' and so on. I'm not a fool, Mandy. I don't believe in that corny old business of 'a wife in name only' either. I'd expect you to *be* a wife. I'd make love to you all day and all night and never give you a moment to think of Jon. I'd make you see you didn't need him. I'd make you want me.'

She opened her mouth to protest, but Mike gave her no chance.

'I know it isn't a very romantic approach, Mandy, but I'm being practical. You're young and warm and loving and, like any other young woman, you need love. The kid has kept you emotionally engaged so far, but that won't last, once you've had time to notice the vacuum you're living in. It won't be long before you'll wake up the needs of that other side of you, if you haven't already. A woman needs loving; needs companionship; needs a man.'

'You may be right, Mike, but I couldn't possibly marry you. You must know that. I don't love you. And despite what you said earlier, it *wouldn't* be fair. Maybe it could have worked out . . . if I wasn't in love with someone else. But you'd know . . . I'd know . . . no, it can't work, Mike, though thank you again for asking me.'

Mike shrugged off the refusal.

'You can't know that it wouldn't work, any more than I can be sure it will work. But I believe it can. Give me a chance to prove it, Mandy. I know you've been up to your eyes in work since you moved in, but that can't go on and you must get time off. Come out with me. Let me prove I can make you happy. Just give me a chance, that's all I'm asking. And if you're thinking of saying 'No', consider the alternative — day in and day out in the same house, getting more and more wretched about Jon. And how long before Gillian guesses the truth? She could, and quite possibly would, make your life hell. That's the kind of situation she'd find amusing. 'Guess what, Patty, Mandy's crazy about Jon. Isn't it a giggle!''

He mimicked Gillian's voice so well, Mandy felt herself shivering. It *would* be horrible. And Mike was right — how long could she hide her feelings?

Suddenly Mike's proposition looked not only possible but desirable. Going out with him, being 'his girl', did not commit her to marriage. He knew the truth as to her feelings for Jon and for himself. She had been alone too long and much as she adored Timmy, a child was not enough.

'If only . . . '

'I know!' Mike broke in roughly. 'If only you didn't love Jon. And if only I could show him up for a right bastard, not worth loving. But I can't do that. I think he's a decent sort of chap and more deserving of you than Gilly. But they are all 'ifs', Mandy. The fact is, he is married to Gillian and he loves her and he isn't the sort to have affairs on the side even if you were. So you've got to go on from there.'

He put his arms round her and kissed her gently. He felt her tautness and then, when he made no move to change from tenderness to passion, he felt her softening, relaxing until she was lying trustingly against him. This, he knew, was the way it would have to be. He must put a strong curb on himself and win her with gentleness and kindness. She might well turn to him on the rebound and, frankly, he didn't care what the reason provided he won her in the end. It was the first time he had ever loved a woman and the first time he had not looked on a woman as a means of fun, amusement, satisfaction. This time he was not taking, but giving, and he knew that it might be a long time before he could expect anything in return.

Gillian drained the last dregs of

champagne from her glass and banged it down on the table in front of her. She was beside herself with frustration and anger that Mike should have rejected her in favour of that insipid little Mandy, too.

She glanced at her husband and felt her irritation mounting. He looked subdued and morose.

'I'm sick to death of this party!' she said in a quiet furious little voice. 'Take me home, Jon. I've had enough.'

With difficulty, Jon managed to control the surge of annoyance that welled up in him.

'I'm sorry if you're bored but we can't exactly break up the party, can we?'

Gillian's eyes narrowed.

'That's typical of you, Jon. It's always what we can and can't do in this crummy little town. Convention! It's all you think about. Who the hell is going to care if we go home now?'

'Since you ask, I mind. Your friends may be as unconventional as you wish to be, Gilly, but I happen to be old-fashioned enough to think good manners are important.'

'For God's sake!' Gillian's eyes were blazing. 'Well, if you won't take me, I'll get a taxi. You can make some suitably conventional excuse for me,' she added sarcastically.

'Gilly, please!' Jon drew a deep breath. He was still far from fully recovered from the 'flu and simply did not feel up to a domestic row. Apart from the unpleasantness of a quarrel at any time, this was the beginning of a new year and it seemed terrible that he and Gilly should be starting it off with a row. He had had such high hopes for this evening. Gilly had seemed in an excellent mood earlier in the day and had, at his request, moved her belongings back from the dressing room into their bedroom. He'd missed her warm body beside him in the big double bed; had missed the pleasure of watching her undress and go through her nightly ritual of removing her make-up and preparing for the night. He had been lonely, especially so since she had avoided the sickroom for fear of germs and he'd seen so little of her since Christmas.

'I said I want to go home!' Gillian was reminding him in a hard determined voice. 'Is that such an unreasonable request from a wife to her husband? There was a time when I wouldn't have had to ask twice,' she added meaningfully.

He caught her meaning at once, but he couldn't accept the implication that she wanted to be home alone with him. He realised she was childishly put out because Mike had been paying attention to Mandy instead of to her and knew, from past experience, that Gillian's mood was always hard and cruel when her wishes were frustrated. He tried to make allowance for the fact that she'd been spoilt all her life and he had failed in so many ways to give her the kind of life she wanted. He excused her selfishness, her egotism, her vanity because they were the results of her extraordinary beauty and her upbringing. He believed that in time Gillian's true nature would overcome her weaknesses and that love would soften, gentle her. Perhaps that was the answer now; that she needed him to restore her ego!

Nevertheless, he could not feel free to abandon the party to which he was host.

Gillian, watching his face, sensed his thoughts.

'We've every reason to go. It's after midnight and you've been ill. No one would think it odd or rude.'

No matter what means she employed, Gillian was determined to go. She would not be humiliated by Mike one moment longer. She'd seen him leave the room, his arm round Mandy's shoulders like some love-sick schoolboy! No doubt he'd found some place where he could make love to the girl. How blind she had been, believing Mike was continually round at the house to see her, Gillian. She'd been nothing more than an excuse for him to make time with that two-faced little . . .

'What about Mandy?' Jon was saying. 'If we leave, how will she get home?'

Gillian gave a brittle laugh.

'My dear Jon, you're really not with it at all, are you? Can't you see what's going on right under your nose? Mike's on the make and has been for ages. If we're not careful, we're going to have another dear little bastard on our hands!'

'Gilly!' Jon's voice was trembling with anger. 'That is a disgusting thing to say and quite unfounded, not to say prejudiced. Just because . . . '

'Oh, shut up, Jon!' Gillian interrupted furiously. 'I'm sick to death of having that girl pushed down my throat as a model of Ideal Woman. Let's face a few facts for once. She's a tramp and she has the kid to prove it and what she can do once, she can do again. Just because she nursed you like some imitation Florence Nightingale, you seem to think she's an angel of purity or something like it. Why, she'd probably go to bed with you if you gave her half a chance. She thinks you're God as it is!'

Jon felt his face redden with embarrassment. He remembered with sudden sickening clarity the way Mandy had felt when he danced with her; the way her body had responded to his; the way she had returned his kiss. Mandy had been warm, passionate and responsive. Yet he would never have thought of her in Gillian's terms had Gilly not put the idea into his head. He felt sickened and somehow ashamed — as if the innocence of their relationship had never existed. He'd known without conscious thought that Mandy was devoted to him, just as he had become attached to her. But until tonight, on the dance floor, he'd never once thought of her as a woman who could attract him, be attracted by him.

'Do you have to spoil everything?' he asked Gillian bitterly.

Jock and Patty were leaving the dance

floor and coming towards their table. Gillian saw them and stood up.

'Well, are you going to take me home or aren't you?' she asked Jon. 'I'm leaving, whatever you do!'

Exhausted, Jon stood up and nodded.

'I'll take you home,' he said. 'I've no wish to stay!'

Gillian made their excuses facilely enough. Jon did look ill and was beginning to feel it. When they reached the house he declined Gillian's suggestion that they should have a nightcap and went straight up to bed. When Gillian joined him a quarter of an hour later he was nearly asleep.

Gillian's mood had changed. A double whisky on top of the champagne at the party had made her slightly drunk. She went over to the bed and flopped down on it beside Jon, giggling softly.

'Don't you go to sleep on me!' she said provocatively. 'That's not what we came home for, remember?'

Tired though he was, Jon felt the

familiar magic of Gilly's seduction work its customary response in him. It was not often, these days, that she made the advances. All too often he had been the one to ask and Gilly the one to reject. He did not understand her. As she began her ritual of undressing and he lay watching her, he knew that he had never understood her and that this had been part of the fascination she had for him. He had never really possessed her. The phrase 'her beauty enslaved him' wandered through his exhausted mind and seemed to have some important message. But love — had she ever really loved him? Did she love him now? Or was she merely hungry for the love-making that had had to be denied whilst he'd been ill? And did it matter? Wasn't it enough that she was slipping into bed beside him, all her beauty his now to hold and possess?

He began to kiss her, and briefly, not for long, he remembered that other mouth he had kissed tonight; those soft, tender receptive lips that had swept him from pity to desire in one short moment. Then he forgot as Gillian's passionate demands claimed and possessed him, draining him of all emotion, even desire.

The following morning they woke to snow and icy temperatures. The atmosphere inside the house was only a little less chilly. Gillian did not put in an appearance until after eleven and was irritable and barely civil when she wandered into the surgery. Mandy was alone. But for her curiosity, Gillian would not have spoken to Mandy at all.

'What time did lover-boy bring you home?' she asked, her voice heavy with sarcasm.

'Soon after two,' Mandy said truthfully. Mike had, at her request, dropped her at the door and made no attempt to detain her. Unexpectedly, she had fallen asleep almost instantly, but she had had only four hours' sleep, for Timmy had woken her, as was his custom, soon after six. She felt tired and nervy and in no mood to cope with Gillian's hangover.

Jon, too, had been up early, but, other than a brief good morning at the breakfast table, had been distant and unusually curt, which had puzzled and distressed her. Gillian was eying her speculatively.

'Don't you think it might be a good idea for you to get Jon to put you on the Pill?' she said viciously.

Mandy felt her nerves snap. Furiously, she retorted:

'And don't you think it might be a good idea to mind your own business?'

Surprisingly, Gillian laughed.

'So the kitten has claws! I'd never have believed it of you, Mandy. To tell you the truth, you're far more amusing when you've lost your temper than when you're playing Miss Meek-and-Mild. I simply can't wait to tell Jon . . . '

'Tell me what?' Jon asked from the doorway. He felt tired and depressed and had been hoping desperately that he would not find Gilly in a bad mood.

It was a relief to hear her laugh as he entered the room.

'Darling, you'll never guess. Our docile little Mandy has just lost her temper. I bet you didn't know she had one!'

Jon felt his muscles stiffen. Despite every intention to the contrary, his eyes were drawn to Mandy's face and he was horrified to see that she looked on the brink of tears. He ignored Gillian's remark.

'Gilly, Mandy's got work to do. I came to see if you'd be able to rustle me up a cup of coffee. Any hope?'

Gilly shrugged.

'I suppose there'll be some in the kitchen.'

She was bored again. Jon had not taken up cudgels in Mandy's defence and the fun of baiting Mandy had lost its flavour. She wandered off to make the coffee.

Mandy bent over her desk, her hair hiding her face, her fingers gripping the pen to stop them trembling. She knew

Jon was standing watching her and was afraid if he spoke to her kindly she would burst into tears.

'Gilly's not very proficient with the percolator,' she said in a small, controlled voice. 'Perhaps you ought to give her a hand.'

Jon hesitated a moment longer. As Gilly's husband, he knew he ought not to criticise her to Mandy, yet he knew only too well how hurtful she could be when she was in one of her sarcastic nasty moods. If Mandy really had lost her temper, Gilly must have been pretty awful and he longed to apologise for her, to bring a smile back to Mandy's face. Her unhappiness engulfed him and he was powerless to cope with it. Gilly's moods were beginning to get him down. Even the passion shared last night had lost its power to keep him feeling tender and gentle towards her this morning. She seemed to have been more difficult since Mandy had come to live with them, yet he could see no reason why. Mandy relieved her of many of the chores she found so boring. Certainly he, himself, could not possibly have coped without Mandy. He simply would not entertain the idea of asking Mandy to leave, even though Gillian seemed to have taken a dislike to her.

'I expect we are all a bit under the weather this morning,' he said vaguely by way of an apology. 'I'll get you some coffee.'

As he was leaving the room the telephone rang. Mandy lifted the receiver and heard Mike's friendly voice:

'Happy New Year, darling!' He sounded happy and full of fun. 'How are you? Where are you? What are you doing and will you lunch with me? And, by the way, I love you.'

Mandy felt herself relax.

'You are an idiot!' she said smiling. 'And Happy New Year to you, too. To answer all your questions, I'm in the surgery, working, busy and I can't possibly lunch with you as you very well know. Moreover, I'm not off duty until seven-thirty this evening.'

Mike gave an exaggerated snort.

'Then I'll report you to your union, tell them you're doing too much overtime. If you can't lunch, better still, dine with me.'

Mandy hesitated. Mike was good for her. The tensions in the house were unbearable, yet she did not feel inclined to ask Gillian a favour and if she were to go out to dinner with Mike someone would have to baby-sit for Timmy.

'I'd really like to, Mike, but not tonight. I think I ought to get to bed early. I'm feeling the effects of last night.'

'Then I'll promise to have you home by ten. How's that?'

'I'd rather leave it till tomorrow. Would that be okay?'

'Whatever you say, darling. All the same, I can't last twenty-four hours without seeing you. I'll drop by at drinks time. Tell Gilly I'll bring a bottle with me.'

He rang off before she could talk him out of it. Somehow she didn't think Gillian would give Mike a very good reception.

When Jon returned with a cup of coffee for her she had herself under control. She forced a smile as she took the cup and saucer from him and was gratified to see the look of apprehension leave his face. She began to talk about work and within minutes the old easy relationship was re-established between them.

It can work! Mandy told herself when she was alone once more. As long as I don't think of Jon except as a doctor and my employer — and as long as Mike is around to keep me from getting morbid with self-pity. I can get over my love given a little time. I don't *really* love him. I only think I do because he is so kind; because I feel he needs me; because he is a very attractive man and I've been lonely. I'm not really in love at all!

Nevertheless, her fingers remained

clasped firmly round the pencil Jon had been holding and which, unconsciously, she had picked up and clung to, simply because it had been in contact with him.

10

January gave way to February and February to March. Jon was back at work, the pressure eased as the extreme cold killed off the 'flu germs and the epidemic petered out. Miss Hill was in a convalescent home, still far from well, and Mandy had agreed to take on the job permanently. Her decision, she was well aware, sprang from weakness. As long as Jon needed her, she couldn't leave him, although Mike had continually pressed her to go away and make a fresh start, promising his support and as anxious as ever to marry her and give her and Timmy a home.

Perhaps, she told herself, she would have found the strength of will to leave if only Jon had been happy. But his relationship with Gilly seemed to deteriorate every day and it was impossible, living at such close quarters, for Mandy to close her eyes and ears to the constant nagging Gilly subjected him to. It was as if Gilly deliberately wished to humiliate her husband by getting at him in front of her, Mandy. Jon never retaliated and even Mike had been forced to comment that it was time Jon straightened Gilly out or he'd end up in a mental home.

Neither Mandy nor Mike were aware of the cause for Gilly's increasingly cruel behaviour or for Jon's tolerance. Gilly was pregnant.

'I'm not having it!' she had stormed and railed at Jon. 'You've got to get rid of it. You're a doctor. Do something. I *won't* have it.'

Jon had done his utmost to persuade her that she would feel differently once the first few months were passed and she was feeling less sick and became accustomed to the idea.

'I'll see you have the very best gynaecologist. You won't have any pain, darling, when your time comes, I promise.'

'My time is not *going* to come!' Gillian shouted back. 'I told you I wasn't having kids and I'm not. It's all your fault. You ought to have thought about it that New Year's Eve. Well, now you'd better do something about it and quick. If you won't, I'll find a clinic in London that will.'

'I won't let you kill our child, Gilly. I want the baby even if you don't. You're young and healthy, and there's no reason why you shouldn't have it. Darling, please, for my sake . . . '

'I'm not having it, Jon, and that's that!'

Jon's face had tightened stubbornly.

'I know you are legally entitled to an abortion, Gilly, but in your case there is no reason to have one; no risk to your mental or physical health and no risk of the baby being abnormal. So please, darling, put such ideas out of your mind.' His voice softened. 'After all, why *not* have a baby? It isn't as if

you've a career that would be interrupted or even a job you'd have to give
up. A baby would give you something to
do.'

'I'll get rid of it somehow, Jon. If you
won't help me, I'll find someone who
will!'

But Gillian's enquiries were far from
encouraging. A one-time model girl-
friend of hers knew of a private clinic
where she could go, but said she would
need at least two hundred pounds for
expenses. She did not have such a sum
in her account. She always overspent on
her allowance and had quite a large bill
owing to the dress shop where she
bought most of her clothes. There was
only her father to appeal to but for
some idiotic reason he called 'his
principles', he refused ever to give her
more cash when she asked for it. Nor
would she dare tell him the reason why
she needed it.

She went up to London and had a
pregnancy test which, as she feared,
proved positive. With no further doubt

as to the necessity to do something quickly, she asked Geoff for a loan. He looked embarrassed as well as surprised.

'I know it's none of my business, Gilly, but why me? I mean, won't Jon help you out if you're short of cash?'

Gillian bit her lip.

'I don't want Jon to know why I want the money,' she said flatly. 'I wouldn't have asked you, Geoff, if I hadn't been desperate. You'll get it back, I promise.'

'I see. Well . . . the fact is, Gilly, I'd honestly rather not. I mean, Jon would have my guts for garters if he discovered I'd given you money for something he disapproved of and I do have to live in the same town as he does. Can't you tell me what it's for? Perhaps if I understood the reason . . . '

When Gillian eventually told him he looked even more embarrassed.

'I'm afraid you'll have to count me out, sweetie. You see, our family is part Irish and we're all R.Cs. Abortion is against the specific ruling of the Pope and I couldn't . . . '

Furiously, Gillian had stormed out of the house. She had thought of asking Patty's help, but could see now that it would be pointless. She decided to renew her efforts to persuade Jon to change his mind. She'd give him one month to do so and then, if the worst came to the worst, she'd go to the private clinic and let them send Jon the bill! She renewed her pleading and cajoling and then, when Jon remained adamant, changed her tactics and began deriding him, criticising him, making him look ridiculous whenever she could, determined that if she was suffering, he would, too. She'd break him somehow.

Jon became desperate. He sensed Gillian's ruthless determination to get rid of their child and her growing hatred for him, the one person who stood between her and her will not to have a baby. He was beginning to wonder whether he had the right to insist she had a baby she did not want.

All babies had the right to be born wanted. Yet he could not bear the thought of having his child, so long desired, destroyed as if it were nothing.

The sight of Mandy's Timmy affected him with conflicting feelings of longing and despair. If only Gillian had Mandy's temperament! But he knew that kind of reasoning led nowhere.

If Gilly kills our child, I'll hate her for the rest of my life! he thought. He was no longer sure if he still loved her. The effort to be understanding, gentle, tolerant, was becoming daily more and more difficult. He was afraid his own mental state was becoming affected. Bringing other women's babies into the world had become a minor form of torture where once it had been nothing but joy.

Nor was time on his side. He knew that after twelve weeks the termination of a pregnancy could be dangerous and ever more so as the weeks went by. He couldn't sit back and wait for Gilly to change her mind in case she never did so. He was hopelessly torn between his professional and his personal opinion.

Gillian, watching her husband closely, sensed the weakening and redoubled her efforts. She changed her tactics and began again to appeal to him.

'It's as much for your sake as for mine, Jon. Think how a yelling brat would spoil our life together. Instead of there being just you and me free to do as we please when we please, we'd be tied the way Mandy is with that kid of hers; up at six in the morning; can't go out because there's no baby-sitter. You *know* we'd both hate it. We don't have nearly enough time together as it is, with your work getting in the way. We were so happy together before this happened, darling. Let's be happy again, the way we used to be.'

Silently Jon had considered what Gilly chose to call the 'happy days of the past'. Had he been happy? Had Gilly herself been happy? She had been bored and resentful of their life together. A child might somehow have brought them closer together — made the bare bones of the marriage into a real flesh-and-blood union. In this painful moment of facing the truth he could see that there had been little else but sex to hold them together; no real understanding or sympathy or companionship; no shared interests — nothing beyond the pleasures of the big double bed.

Suddenly he knew that Gilly had won. He simply did not care any more what happened. His marriage was and always had been a farce. His wife did not care in the slightest what he felt, what he needed, what he wanted. She was, and always had been, concerned only with herself. His love, like his seed, had fallen on stony ground and could never grow to fruition.

'You do what you want, Gilly. I just don't care any more!'

Triumphant, Gillian did not look deeper into the meaning of his surrender. Even had she realised she had finally lost Jon's love, she wouldn't have cared. Nothing mattered but that she was free to get rid of the unwanted child.

'Jon, that's the most marvellous thing you ever said to me!' she cried, unaware of the bitterness that flooded his face. 'I'll fix everything. You've nothing to worry about except a bit of money. I'll need a few hundred pounds. Oh, darling, I'm so happy. I think this is the happiest day of my whole life.'

Jon nodded and turned quickly away, lest she should see the expression on his face. He knew that somehow he had to get over this emotion; of hating her as much as he once loved her. No matter what she did, she was still his wife and he would have to continue living with her. He must get a grip on himself and learn to accept the truth. But for the time being he knew that he wanted to run as far away from her as possible; not to have to see her; not to have to hear her voice; not ever again to have to think about the child that would never be born.

* * *

Working almost side by side with Jon, it was impossible Mandy should not see the sudden shocking apathy that enveloped him. At first she thought he might be ill again, but he denied he was unwell and in so frigid a manner that he forbade further enquiries. Sensitive to his every mood, she became painfully aware of his equally sudden and inexplicable rejection of Timmy. Where in the past he had always found time to play with the little boy after tea, to go to his nursery to say good night to him, to smile and talk to him at meals, now he avoided the child, even pushing him aside when Timmy ran to him. Mandy was torn between anger at the rejection of her son and bewilderment as to the cause. Timmy reacted by turning tearful and whining where once he had been all laughs and chatter. That Jon was distant and off-hand with her was hurtful enough, but that he should withdraw his love so totally from

Timmy was unbearable.

Mike, too, noticed. A week after Jon's strange behaviour had begun he called to see Mandy and, finding her alone in the sitting room, as Jon was out on his rounds and Gilly away staying with friends in London, he said bluntly:

'Something's wrong in this house, Mandy. You're looking miserable, Jon's biting everyone's head off, even Timmy's. What's the matter? Do you know?'

Mandy shook her head.

'Did Jon and Gilly have a row? Has she gone off in a huff? Do you think that's what's upsetting him?'

'I don't think so. Gillian had been pretty frightful, as you know, after the New Year dance, but last week she seemed to pull herself together and couldn't have been nicer to Jon. In fact, he was the one who was being touchy, not Gillian. Something's happened to Jon. I don't know what it is. He seems to hate everyone — even Timmy!'

Mike sat down and put an arm round her shoulders.

'Mandy, darling, I just hate to see you so wretched. This isn't a happy house. You ought not to be living here. I know I promised not to propose again for at least six months, but the way things are, you've got to get out of here and I want you to let me take you and Timmy away.'

Mandy stiffened, as he had been afraid she would.

'Mike, I can't go away with you — you know that. Maybe you are right and I ought to take Timmy away from here, for his sake now as well as mine, but you know how I feel about marrying you. I just couldn't do it unless I was in love with you.'

'And you're still in love with Jon!' Mike finished for her, sighing. 'I suppose I knew before I spoke that that's what you'd say. But surely you must see for yourself that there's no future in loving Jon. It's not as if there's the remotest likelihood he'd ever

divorce Gilly, especially now there's a
kid on the way. You can't stay
alone . . . '

'What did you say?' Mandy broke in.
'A baby? Gillian is going to have a
baby? But why didn't she say? Why
didn't Jon say? I didn't know!'

Mike looked embarrassed.

'I suppose I shouldn't have let that
particular cat out of the bag. In fact, it
was very remiss of me. The fact is I
assumed you knew already.'

'But are you sure? How do *you*
know?'

Mike withdrew his arm and busied
himself lighting a cigarette. He looked
suddenly uneasy.

'I'm not sure I ought to say any
more,' he said slowly. 'On the other
hand, maybe I can explain a lot of
things. I never thought of the connection before, but now . . . '

Mandy's face was chalk white as she
stared at him in total disbelief.

'Whatever you know, I want to know,'
she said. 'No matter what it is.'

'Okay, but it isn't very nice. The fact is, Gilly asked Geoff for a cash loan because she was pregnant and wanted an abortion and Jon wouldn't consider it. Geoff refused. Naturally I assumed Gilly had given up the idea but now . . . well, with Jon behaving as if he'd been bulldozed and Gilly gone happily off to London to 'stay with friends', one is forced to wonder if Jon gave in, poor devil.'

'Oh, no!' The words were wrung from her. Jon, who so much loved children, wanted them so badly! Jon, who was dedicated to saving life, having to agree to destroying it.

'Doesn't look too good, does it?' Mike said flatly. 'But I suppose if Gilly really didn't want it . . . Hell, I don't know, Mandy. All I know is that it isn't any of our business and you, in particular, can't get involved. That's one more reason for you leaving here.'

Mandy's chin jutted forward stubbornly.

'How can I walk out on Jon when

he's got this on his mind? Mike, I love him. I've got to be here to do what I can. I've got to!'

'But what can you do? You can't save his child. You can't make Gilly into a different person. You can't remake a rotten marriage. You can't do anything, Mandy, other than torture yourself.'

'I don't matter. It's Jon who . . . '

'You do matter, Mandy. You matter to me, for what that's worth, and you matter a hell of a lot to Timmy. You've got to think of your life now and your future. What Jon and Gilly make of their life is their affair, not yours, not mine. He can get another secretary and that's the only place you've any right to in his life. That may sound hard but it's true.'

Mandy bit deep into her lower lip, which was trembling uncontrollably. Mike was right. She knew it in her heart, yet she could not bear the thought of leaving Jon now, alone as he had never been alone, wretched, tormented and bitter.

'It'll be up to Gilly to make it up to him somehow, if she can,' Mike continued inexorably. 'If Jon were to turn to you for comfort, Mandy, as well he might, you'd only make it harder for him. For his sake, you've got to get away from here, if not for your own.'

He put his arms round her and held her tightly.

'Don't fight the impossible, darling. I do love you, as it happens, very much indeed. Once you make up your mind to go, it won't be so hard. Jon wouldn't make it difficult for you, I'm sure. In fact, he'd want you to be happy.'

'Wouldn't make what difficult?'

Jon's voice, cool but quite clear, brought them both to their feet. Mike kept his arm round Mandy's shoulder, pressing against her to give her the strength he knew she would need if she were not to weaken.

'I want to marry Mandy. I want to take her away from here and give her a home of her own. I was saying that I was sure you'd want her to be happy,

Jon, and that you wouldn't make it difficult for her to leave.'

Jon's eyes went from Mike's to Mandy's. He could read nothing in them but a fear he did not understand. For his own part, he was shattered. Of course he'd known since the New Year that Mike was 'courting' Mandy, had at first teased her about her 'boyfriend', but when she'd told him curtly that she had not the slightest intention of marrying Mike he'd dropped the subject and assumed the two of them were merely friends. It was an inexplicable shock to think of Mandy going away — to marry Mike; taking Timmy away . . . though perhaps in the circumstances that would not be such a bad thing. He could not see Mandy's little boy now without thinking of . . .

'When are you thinking of leaving, Mandy?'

Somehow his voice sounded normal, matter-of-fact. He was surprised and pleased that none of his confusion was showing.

'I don't know. I . . . '

'As soon as you've found a replacement for her,' Mike said steadily. 'She naturally doesn't want to leave you without anyone.'

'It won't be easy to replace you!' Jon said simply, looking at Mandy and trying not to wonder if she really was in love with Mike. Somehow it seemed impossible. She'd given no indication, ever, that she cared deeply for the young man. Surely he would have noticed if she'd been anything but casual? Not that he had noticed very much lately, with his mind so gripped with other things. Maybe whilst he had been engrossed in his own unhappiness Mandy had found her happiness. He must try somehow to appear pleased, happy, glad for them both.

'My congratulations!' he said stiffly. 'Is the engagement official?'

Mike's 'Yes' and Mandy's 'No' came out simultaneously. Jon's eyes narrowed. So Mandy wasn't as much in a hurry as Mike!

'Mandy naturally doesn't want to seem ungrateful, what with you giving her and Timmy a home and so on. She won't come away with me until she feels you'll be able to cope without her!'

Jon's mouth took on a bitter twist.

'Ah, so it's duty before pleasure. Well, my dear girl, put your mind at rest. No one, but no one, is indispensable. I can find another secretary, albeit not so efficient or dedicated to duty as yourself!'

The sarcasm of his tone was more wounding even than his words. Hurt beyond bearing and feeling both defeated and humiliated, Mandy tore herself away from Mike, and, pushing past Jon, ran out of the room.

Mike said impulsively:

'You didn't have to hurt her, Jon!'

Jon stared at him uncomprehendingly.

'Hurt her? I didn't intend to. How could I?'

'Because she's in love with you!'

Mike said, turning away and walking over to the window. 'I suppose you hadn't any idea and I'm not blaming you. But it's better you should know the truth because she can't go on living here like this for the rest of her life. So let her go. *Make* her go. I love her and I'll take care of her . . . and Timmy.'

'Oh, God! What a bloody awful mess!' Jon said, sitting down heavily and covering his eyes with his hands. 'I didn't realise. I honestly didn't realise. I'd do anything in the world rather than hurt her. Mandy's meant one hell of a lot to me. The way I feel about her . . . well, she's someone special, someone I like and respect and admire. I've valued her friendship, her loyalty, her help, her sympathy. I never realised . . . '

'It doesn't matter now, Jon. The only thing that matters is her future happiness. There isn't a future for her here and I want to get her away. She won't go if she thinks you need her. At least promise me you won't let her know you'll miss her.'

'My God, I will, though! I've grown to rely on her, depend on her. She's all I've . . . ' He bit back the remainder of the sentence, but too late for Mike not to guess the end of it. With Mandy and Timmy gone, there'd be nothing but hate left in the house, the hate he had for Gilly and the marriage that was rotten to the core, just as Gilly was rotten.

'I'm sorry!' Mike said gently. 'I really am, Jon. But let her go.'

'Yes, of course!' Jon said slowly.

For a long time after Mike had left, he sat alone, wondering what life in this house would be like, with no Mandy, no Timmy, and devoid of love.

11

My dear Jon,

You will see from the address that I have left the Nursing Home and am staying with Father. Naturally I haven't told him the real nature of my operation and I've written to most of our friends and said it was an appendix removal, so you needn't worry about anyone finding out the truth.

I suppose you won't be surprised to hear that it was a very unpleasant ordeal and I'm still far from fit. Father says I can stay here a couple of weeks to convalesce as I'm not fit to come home to domestic chores. No doubt the efficient Mandy will continue to cope as always.

I suppose you've been as busy as usual but I do think you might have written or phoned. After all, darling, *it was all rather depressing and as you were the cause of it all, the least you could have done was send flowers and sympathy or whatever. I had to borrow some cash from Father to pay the bill which was a bit more expensive than I'd worked out but well worth every penny, don't you agree? I know you weren't keen on the idea but I'm sure now it's all over, you'll be as pleased as I am.*

I'm expecting friends in for tea so no more now. Do ring me one evening. Father thinks it a bit odd when no mail or phone call comes from you.

Ever your loving,
Gilly

Jon put the letter in the wastepaper basket. He was interviewing Mandy's replacement in five minutes' time and he needed those five minutes to steel himself against rejecting the young woman who'd applied for the job. Mandy had told him the girl's qualifications were

262

excellent — she'd been both a typist and a dental nurse and, at thirty, wanted a more varied and responsible post. Mandy had liked her, but Jon knew in advance he wasn't going to like anyone sitting in Mandy's chair, bringing his coffee, dealing with his patients. He had, somehow, to rid himself of this bias and stop his feeling that the end of the world had come because Mandy was leaving.

His reaction to Mike's announcement that Mandy was in love with him had at first been that of incredulity. But this had been followed almost at once by comprehension and a terrible feeling of regret. But for Gillian and his fateful marriage, he could all too easily have returned Mandy's love. In a way, he did love her. It was far from the same obsessional attraction that had drawn him to Gilly. What he felt for Mandy he had already described to Mike, an innate liking and respect and sympathy. There was, and always had been, the desire to protect her and help her. He had and still did truly love Timmy, not so much because he was Pete's child but because he was Mandy's. He had discovered these last few days that he was desperately envious of Mike . . . and jealous, too. He hated to see the possessive way Mike put his arm round her, kissed her, looked at her.

Gillian's letter neither surprised nor distressed him. He noted with a kind of factual disinterest that he was, temporarily anyway, emotionally immune to her. She'd lost the power to hurt him.

Her next letter, following two days later, did at least arouse him to anger.

My dear Jon,

You may think you are being very clever ignoring me in this way but Father's opinion of you is unrepeatable. In fact, he says your treatment of me is not far short of mental cruelty. I don't understand you and it's obvious you don't understand me. I was feeling very loving and tender towards you but that's rapidly wearing thin. I know you wanted the baby but you did agree we should get rid of it so you can't blame me now, if that's what you're trying to do. I'm getting fed up with your selfishness and your lack of consideration for my feelings. What do you imagine my friends think? I've told everyone you'll be coming up next weekend to fetch me so you'd better make arrangements to do so. And don't say you're too busy as you are due for a holiday and that old fool Dr Harvey, can hold the fort on Saturday and Sunday.

I'm warning you here and now, Jon, not to try my patience too far. If you want me back then you'd better start showing it in person.

Love,
Gilly

His first reaction of anger was followed almost at once by pity. Poor spoilt little girl! Even now, when she had hurt him more deeply than he could have believed possible for a wife to hurt her husband, she was still petulantly complaining at *his* selfishness, his lack of understanding, and consideration; even issuing threats.

'*If you want me back*' she had written, never once doubting that he would want her. Yet he could not bring himself to care whether or not she ever came back. It just did not seem to matter one way or another. Much more urgently his mind was on the thought of Mandy's departure in two weeks' time. He'd engaged the new girl, neither liking nor disliking her, doing so in order to give Mandy her freedom and because he knew if he allowed his own personal wishes to come to the fore, he'd reject any replacement.

Gilly's third letter was not even a veiled threat.

If you don't come for me at the weekend, I shall not come home at all, so think carefully, Jon, before you go too far. I imagine you don't want a divorce but I will not be made to suffer like this because I had a perfectly legal abortion . . .

He wrote back, not because her threats frightened him but because he wanted to keep the record straight.

I'm not trying to 'punish' you, Gilly. The reason I haven't written is because there did not seem anything suitable to say in the circumstances. As for coming to collect you at the weekend, Dr Harvey is ill and I am quite truthfully unable to leave, as you'll appreciate. If you are not well enough to come by train, perhaps you should stay another week with your father until you are quite fit.

Gillian flung the letter across the breakfast table to her father.

'Just read that!' she stormed. 'That'll show you how much he cares for me!'

The old man picked up the letter and read it slowly. Then he peered at his daughter over his spectacles.

'Not exactly a Valentine card, but to the point. I really don't understand what this tiff is about, Gilly. It doesn't make sense to me. Jon has always cared about you — and you know it — far more than you ever cared about him. If his love has turned to indifference, and that's the tone of his letter, you must have upset him somehow. I never saw any young husband more in love with his wife than Jon was with you. You've hurt him somehow.'

He noticed the two bright spots of colour on Gillian's cheeks and added shrewdly:

'I suppose that *was* an appendicitis operation you had, my girl, and not something far more consequential?'

'I don't know what you're talking about. I had my appendix out!' Gillian lied furiously.

'Well, I'm not going to question that statement again, Gilly, because if the other were the case, I'd feel forced to side with Jon. I'd have liked a grandson and I'm old-fashioned enough to disapprove of the newfangled laws on the destruction of life. So I'll not probe too deep, but I'll advise you to tread very warily. You could go too far with a man like Jon.'

Gillian scowled.

'I don't know that I want *him* any more. I'm bored to death down there. I positively loathe being a doctor's wife. And don't say you warned me. You never told me that it was going to be like it is!'

'You might be less bored if you had a child or two!' her father replied pointedly. 'And I suggest you think twice about divorcing Jon. It's doubtful you could prove mental cruelty and even if you could, there's precious little alimony in the kitty, as you well know.'

Gillian got up and walked round the table. She looked very young and innocent in a flowered Laura Ashley print dress. For a moment her father's heart softened as she put her arms round him and placed her smooth warm cheek against his own.

'Don't you ever miss having me around, Daddy?' she asked childishly. 'Don't you get lonely here by yourself?'

He untangled her arms and said gruffly:

'I'm not going to help you bust your marriage, Gilly, by offering you a comfortable bolt-hole here with me. You made your bed and you'd best lie in it — that is, if Jon still wants you. Bored or not, your place is with him and I'll not keep you here.'

Gillian went home by train at the weekend. Jon, it appeared, had no intention of sharing his bed with her. He had moved his belongings into the dressing room. She pretended not to notice, sure of her powers of seduction when the right moment came.

Nor did he return her kiss as she greeted him with a bright 'I'm back, darling!' He turned away and said:

'There's been quite a lot happening since you left. For one thing, Mandy and Mike have become engaged and, for another, Mandy leaves in two weeks' time and I've a new girl taking her place. I hope you'll get on with her.'

'Mandy *leaving!*' Gillian was shocked into normality. 'But she'd never leave you, Jon. She positively adores you!'

'Don't be silly!' Jon said sharply. 'She's going to marry Mike!'

Gillian threw her suitcase on to the bed and laughed derisively.

'You're the one being silly. Mandy is no more in love with Mike than I am. Anyway Mike isn't the marrying type.'

'He's marrying Mandy!' Jon said again. 'Whether you like it or not!'

'Oh, don't start a quarrel, for heaven's sake!' Gilly said lightly. 'Here I am, home in the very best of moods and you acting like a bear with a sore head. Honestly, darling, I'm dreadfully sorry you're losing your little Florence Nightingale, but it's scarcely the end of the world, is it?'

Her words stayed in his mind as he set off on his afternoon rounds. The end of the world. Perhaps not. Yet it was the end of something. An epoch? No, of an experience. Since Mandy and Timmy had come to live with them, he and Gilly had somehow grown further and further apart. It was as if in total innocence Mandy had somehow drawn attention to all that was lacking in his wife: the sweetness, the warmth, the selflessness, the gentleness, the maternal.

Jon gripped the steering wheel of his car more tightly. This was no way to be thinking. If he let himself draw comparisons such as these he'd end up believing not just that Mandy loved him but that he loved her. It was ridiculous, impossible, absolutely impossible. Gilly was home and she was his wife and somehow they'd got to pick up the threads and make their marriage work. He mustn't go on blaming her. She couldn't help being the way she was. He'd married her knowing she was only a spoilt child but wanting her all the same. It wasn't fair to blame her now because she wasn't a real woman. A woman like . . .

Thankfully, the car had taken him to his first house call and work put an end to thoughts that were dangerous and far, far better left at the very back of his mind, unadmitted, unexpressed.

★   ★   ★

Two weeks later Mandy left. Through his firm, Mike had found her a small flat in the adjoining village. The rent was reasonable and Mandy, in the capacity of secretary-receptionist at his estate agency, was able to afford it. Mike collected her and Timmy and drove them to their new home in his car. Thankfully, Jon was not around, so Mandy did not have the final agony of a goodbye. Gillian waved her a casual farewell and called after them:

'Be good, children, and don't do anything I wouldn't do!' which somehow, by its very brashness, made the going easier for Mandy.

Gillian's attitude also made it easier

for Jon when he returned home that evening.

'Florence Nightingale departed with the gallant Mike and Tiny Tim after lunch,' she told him. 'I imagine they'll be all tucked up in Mandy's flat by now. Wonder whether Mike's made love to her yet. Bet he has, though you never know with Mandy. There was a puritanical streak in the girl I never understood. Sexless, probably. Frigid, anyway.'

Somehow it did not seem to be Mandy she was talking about and Jon felt nothing but a brief tug at his heartstrings when he saw a discarded fire-engine of Timmy's lying in a dark corner on the stairs.

He had made up his mind that the past was going to stay that way, forgotten, unimportant. It was the future that mattered, his and Gilly's; between them they'd got to put their marriage back on its feet. He found he was able to talk to her quietly, without cynicism or bitterness; to discuss a party she wanted to go to, a new colour scheme for the spare room she had decided to decorate. Geoff and Patty came in to dinner one evening and they played bridge and drank whisky. It seemed as if they were returning slowly to normal. It could have worked, Jon told himself, if Gillian hadn't rushed things. One night, flushed with whisky, she had come to the dressing room and sat seductively on the side of his bed.

'It's lonely in that big room all by myself!' she said, looking at him through her lashes. 'Don't think I don't appreciate you moving in here after I'd been ill, but there's really no need to *stay* here, darling, as if you'd been banished!'

She bent over and kissed him. Involuntarily, his muscles stiffened and she noticed and smiled secretively.

'It's been a long time, hasn't it?' she said softly. 'I've missed you, darling. Have you missed me, too?'

This, he told himself, is part of marriage; I've no right to reject her.

That would be cruel. She's very lovely, very desirable. If I stop thinking . . .

Gillian eased herself into the narrow bed beside him and switched off the light. He was grateful. Somehow he felt it would be easier in the dark where she could not see his face, his eyes . . .

'You're so tense, darling!' her voice whispered in his ear. 'Relax and stop worrying that silly old head of yours!' She put her arms around him and he felt her soft hands against his chest. He knew that if he kept his mind dead, his body would respond. But she spoke.

'There's nothing to worry about, sweetie. I had them fix me up in the nursing home so I couldn't conceive again — at least, not till they untie the knot. So you've no need to hold back. We're safe. No matter what we do, we can't have a baby now.'

He tried to make love to her, but inevitably he failed. For a while Gillian was patient and made every effort to arouse him. For his own sake now, as well as for hers, he wanted to be able to play his part. To be impotent was to be only half a man and he, who had never in his life feared it, was impotent now.

Gillian's patience turned to icy anger. She sat up, switched on the light and stared at him with huge flashing eyes.

'Very clever, I don't think! I call it a horrid way to get your own back. Lead me on and then . . . then refuse . . . '

'Gillian, I'm not getting revenge. I'm not refusing. Try and understand. I just can't!'

Gillian gave a furious denial.

'*You* say you *can't?* Don't make me laugh. I know you, Jon. You can if you want and you don't fool me. You *don't* want. Well, I do and if you're not man enough to satisfy me, I'll find some man who is!'

She was out of bed now, her hand on the door-knob.

'You make a big mistake, Jon, if you think you're the only man who can make love the way I like. There's Geoff Sinclair, for one. You can enjoy your little bit of revenge thinking of where

I'll be for the rest of the night — in Geoff's bed.'

'Gillian . . . '

But she did not stay to hear him out. He lay back against the pillows and lit a cigarette. His first reaction of humiliation began to wear off as he tried to sort out logically the reasons for his impotence. It wasn't simply that he no longer loved his wife. A man can find a woman desirable even if he doesn't love her. And Gillian was always desirable in that way. It was her words that had ultimately defeated him; words she had meant to be reassuring when she told him she'd had herself temporarily sterilised. It wasn't simply that he could only make love if he believed they were creating life together. They'd been careful every time until that fateful New Year's Eve. No, it went deeper than that. It was Gillian's total lack of understanding what that unborn baby and its loss meant to him. It was as if she had been trying deliberately to make him face the fact — *no child now or ever if she could help it.* She was offering herself to him on her terms — a marriage based on sex and nothing more. 'We're safe!' she had said, as if they'd been an unmarried couple living in sin and afraid of the consequences. And that was what he felt like.

He wondered if it was his duty to get up and go and prevent her running to Geoff. He wasn't too sure whether she had meant the threat or merely meant to hurt him. Either way, it did not seem a matter for his decision or action so much as for hers. If their marriage really meant anything to her, she wouldn't go. He couldn't, like some Victorian husband, forbid her to go.

He heard the front door slam, heard the sound of the car revving up in the garage. It was possible she was just trying to unnerve him, yet in his heart he didn't think so. She had said: 'You make a big mistake if you think you're the only man who can make love the way I like. There's Geoff Sinclair!' Yes, Geoff would be capable of sitting at his dinner table, drinking his whisky and, the selfsame evening, of making love to his wife. He had a way of looking at Gilly that was certainly covetous, if not possessive. If Gillian's words were to be taken as the truth, she'd already been unfaithful to him with Geoff.

Jon got up and went into the bathroom where he was sick for several minutes. Then he went down to the surgery and found some sleeping pills. He took two in a glass of water, went back to bed and five minutes later fell fast asleep.

12

Mandy sat in the warm sunshine watching Timmy as he played contentedly with another toddler of the same age on the green lawn of the park. It was her half-day and therefore an afternoon she treasured because she could devote herself to the child.

As a rule Mike was with them. He was wonderful with Timmy and seemed to understand instinctively Mandy's need to spend as much time as she could with the boy. If he was jealous of her love for him, Mike certainly never showed it and this was one of the reasons she had finally weakened and agreed to marry him. He genuinely loved Timmy and was more than willing to adopt him after their marriage and take on the responsibilities of a father. In this respect she had no doubts about the rightness of marriage to Mike. The one big flaw was that she still could not fully return the love he lavished on her.

It was now three months since she had walked out of Jon's and Gillian's lives; three months since she had seen Jon. Yet he was never very far from her thoughts. Mike never mentioned his name and neither Geoff nor Patty spoke of the past, as if they had mutually agreed that the least said the better, if Mandy was to forget and make a fresh start as she intended. With Mike so often round at the flat in the evenings and at weekends, and busy as she was during the day working for his estate agency, Mandy had had little time to brood. But in the late hours of darkness her thoughts would invariably wander on the point of sleep beyond her control to painful anguished memories of Jon's unhappy face. All the old torment of her love for him returned to haunt her until sleep brought oblivion.

She had tried not so long ago to confess these secret longings to Mike, but he had shrugged them off as 'inevitable', promising her they were only natural and temporary and would cease in time.

'Once we are married and leading a full married life, it will be different. I want you so desperately, darling. Trust me. It will be all right, I swear it!'

She knew quite well what was at the back of his mind. So far, she had resisted any attempt Mike made to take their relationship a stage further and allow him to stay all night. There were times when, to her own surprise she had been tempted to let him make love to her. She was young, healthy and lonely. It was only natural she should find herself responding physically to Mike's passion. But beyond her physical need was an even stronger desire not to cheat Mike in any way. He had been so wonderful a friend she could not bring herself to take more from him until she felt able to give something in return.

'If you marry me you'll be giving me yourself, Mandy. What more could I want?' he had quibbled. But Mandy knew that the mere legal ceremony he so much wanted could not ensure that she would be able to give him either the love or the response he deserved. Once the first novelty of possession wore off, she was afraid he would realise that the much more vital facet of love was missing. She knew it, even if he did not choose for the moment to recognise the possibility.

But finally she had weakened. It was not just because recently Mike had redoubled his efforts at persuasion. It was her own understanding that the present situation could not continue indefinitely. It was not fair to keep Mike on tenterhooks without any prospects of the situation changing in the future. She knew she must either agree to marry him and allow him to fix a date for their wedding, or else stop seeing him altogether. This last alternative had frightened her. Mike had filled her life completely since she had left Jon's house. It was Mike who had shouldered all the little difficulties of the move, her new job, taking control of her life just as if he were her husband. She had been grateful and glad to lean on him. And apart from an occasional visit to or from Patty and Geoff, she had no other friends, no time to mix with the other young mothers who took their children to the same nursery school Timmy attended. They, too, had jobs and most of them had good homes and husbands to hurry home to. She had Mike waiting to drive her home, help her get Timmy's supper and put him to bed, anxious to have her to himself for a while but always patiently waiting until she had finished doing all she wished to do for the little boy.

I do love him! Mandy thought, as she glanced across the park to see if he were on his way to join them as he had promised when his business appointment was over. He had arranged to collect them and drive them home for tea. But there was no sign of him and

Mandy looked back to see if Timmy was still playing with the other child. He was a happy, mischievous little boy; adventurous, too, and when she could not at first pick him out from amongst the other toddlers, Mandy did not worry. He could not be far away because his fat little legs were incapable of lending him speed even though they gave him some degree of mobility.

She stood up and called him. He was reasonably obedient and usually came when she called. But there was still no immediate sign of him and feeling the first twinge of anxiety, Mandy walked over to the group of mothers supervising the children.

'My little boy — in green denim dungarees and blue jersey — have you seen him?' she asked. 'He was here a moment ago playing with a little girl in a red dress.'

A matronly woman looked up sympathetically from her knitting.

'Take your eyes off 'em for two minutes and they're gone!' she said sighing. 'I don't think I noticed him. How old is he?'

'I think I saw him!'

Mandy turned to the young girl with a pushchair she noticed earlier. 'I think he went off with the little girl in red. They went off towards the rhododendrons!'

'Thank you!' Mandy said gratefully. No doubt Timmy and the little girl were playing hide-and-seek, currently one of Timmy's favourite games.

She hurried across to the clump of rhododendrons, calling Timmy as she half walked, half ran. Two older boys ran out, wearing cowboy suits and carrying cap pistols. She stopped them and questioned them. Neither seemed to have seen the little ones.

She searched a moment longer, but the shrubs were not thick and it soon became clear Timmy was not there. Now her alarm was mounting. She ran back to the group of parents, frantically hoping but without any real hope at all that Timmy would have reappeared amongst them.

'You don't think he could have wandered down to the lake, do you, dear?' the fat woman asked, striking the first real note of terror in Mandy's brain. Timmy was fascinated by the ducks that lived on the ornamental lake and part of the daily ritual was a visit there to throw them bread crusts. The lake was only a few minutes' walk away but hidden by the ornamental pavilion from her present view.

She began to run, praying as she did so that none of the terrible fears now rising hysterically inside her could possibly have any foundation in fact. There would be other people round the pond. Someone would notice a toddler on his own — someone would pull him out if . . .

She saw the group long before they saw her; knew that this was no longer a nightmare of fantasy but a reality. Someone was applying artificial respiration to a small boy dressed in green. Mandy held her breath, unable to ask the impossible question: Is he alive?

The next ten minutes had the unreal quality of a dream. A policeman, summoned earlier when the little boy had first been noticed floating face down on the water, carried Timmy across the grass and paths to where an ambulance stood waiting at the gates. The child lay limp and apparently lifeless, and Mandy, too deeply shocked for words or tears, followed mutely beside him, unaware of the gawping onlookers or of anything beyond the need to get Timmy to hospital as quickly as possible.

The first time she realised there was still hope was when the ambulance men began to give Timmy oxygen. She watched them as they worked in silence, unable to question them for fear of the negative answer they might give. But long before they reached the hospital Timmy had begun to breathe and the men were smiling at her reassuringly and giving her cheerful words that slowly penetrated her numbed mind.

'He'll be okay, you'll see, ma!'

'. . . none the worse in a day or two.'

'Surprising how tough they are at this age for all their smallness . . . '

Timmy was wheeled out of her sight into the care of the casualty doctor. A nurse took Mandy to a waiting room. Another nurse brought her a cup of strong tea she was unable to swallow. A doctor came in, asked if she was Timmy's mother and for details as to his age and other facts which she gave automatically in a small controlled voice giving no inkling to the hysteria lying within her. She wanted to ask how Timmy was, but when the doctor failed to volunteer such information, she felt fear mounting in her again and was afraid to ask.

She closed her eyes and gripped her hands fiercely together. Would someone come and tell her if Timmy had had a relapse? Would they let her see him? Had he really started breathing in the ambulance or had she imagined it? Perhaps the ambulance men were just being kind! How long since she had come in here? How long had they been working on Timmy? What were they doing?

'Mandy? It *is* Mandy, isn't it?'

She felt her hands being gently drawn away from her face. The voice, repeating her name, seemed part of the same impossible dream. It was Jon, holding her tightly by her arms, steadying her as she began to tremble violently with delayed shock.

'Mandy, it's all right. There's nothing to worry about. Don't you understand? *Timmy is all right!* They're putting him to bed in the children's ward and in a few minutes you'll be able to go in and see him. Did you hear what I said, Mandy? He's all right. He's been asking for you!'

She stared up at him unbelievingly. Jon himself wasn't real, so she couldn't believe what he was saying was real, either.

'Darling, stop looking so terrified. The danger's over. Look, Mandy, you'd better come and see Timmy for yourself. You obviously don't believe me!'

But now the gentle teasing tone had convinced her. Jon would never speak banteringly if there were the slightest degree of danger. With the enormity of her relief came the release of tears. He held her, knowing that it was the best thing for her to cry.

When she was calmer he mopped her tears with his handkerchief and reminded her that she could go along to the ward now and see Timmy for herself.

'No, not like this. He might notice I'd been crying!' she said. Only then did the full impact of Jon's presence hit her.

'Why are you here?' she asked, drawing away from his arms, of which she had only just become conscious. 'I don't understand!'

He took her hand and held it.

'I am a doctor, remember?' he said with a smile. 'I was in the hospital seeing a patient of mine and I overheard Sister telling one of the nurses to take 'Timmy's mother' a cup of tea. I pricked up my ears because of the name, wondering if it possibly *could* be your Timmy. Sister put me in the picture, so, of course, I knew it must be you and I came at once. I'm glad I was here. It must have been a terrible ordeal for you.'

Mandy continued to stare at him speechless. He looked so familiar and yet somehow different — thinner, older, perhaps, but still Jon, the man she had tried so hard to forget, so hopelessly to stop loving.

He, in turn, studied Mandy's face — blotched by her tears, yet to him still as beautiful as ever. He'd known for several months that he loved her desperately; just as he had known that such a love was hopeless. She was engaged to Mike Sinclair and shortly to marry him.

Abruptly, as the thought hit him like a sharp pain, he let go of Mandy's hand and said briskly:

'Let me take you along to the ward now, Mandy. Timmy will settle down better if you're there. Come, I'll show you the way.'

She went with him, her legs feeling trembly and weak, which Jon seemed to realise, for he kept an arm beneath hers, supporting her. The children's ward looked bright and cheerful. By the look of it, the patients had not long finished their tea, or was it supper? Mandy's eyes searched the cots. Timmy was in a far corner of the ward, a nurse sitting beside him. He looked very small and very still, but as she approached, the nurse looked up smiling and said:

'He's fast asleep — just dropped off as if nothing had happened. Do you want to stay with him for a little while?'

'I don't think there's much point if he's just gone off,' Jon broke in. 'His mother has had quite a shock herself. Let me run you home, Mandy. I'll give you a sedative and then you can come back this evening and you'll be here if Timmy wakes up.'

Beyond making any decisions for herself, Mandy allowed him to take her out to his car.

'What about your patient?' she asked inconsequently.

'Oh, she's fine. You're the one I'm worried about. Home and bed for you, my girl.'

She seemed unable to stop shivering. Jon told her reassuringly that this was just shock. She gave him directions to her flat and without deferring to her wishes he insisted on taking her up. He took the key away as her shaking hands fumbled with the lock and carried her into her bedroom, laying her on the bed and pulling a duvet round her. Then he disappeared.

When he returned he was carrying a hot-water bottle and a glass of brandy.

'Didn't know you'd taken to drink!' he said cheerfully as he helped her into a sitting position and made her drink it.

She managed to smile.

'It's not really mine, it's Mike's!' she said.

Jon's face tightened. He knew about Mike, yet her words had nevertheless come as a shock.

'You're going to marry Mike, aren't you?' he said as matter of factly as he could manage. 'When's the big day?'

Mandy, too, tried to speak normally as she said:

'In a fortnight's time. How . . . how did you know?'

Jon turned away.

'Gillian wrote and told me. I gather she had the news from Geoff.'

'Gillian *wrote?* Then isn't she at home?' The questions were out before she realised she had no right to ask them. Jon was staring at her with a face full of surprise.

'At my house? But no! Surely you know — Gillian left me two months ago. She went back to live with her father. We're getting divorced.'

'Divorced?' Mandy repeated stupidly. 'I didn't know. No one told me. I thought . . . I thought you and Gillian were . . . '

'Reconciled? No! I think there's only hope of mending a marriage that has hit a rocky patch if the marriage was a good one to begin with. Gillian and I . . . we were never suited. I suppose I always knew it, but I didn't want to accept it. I ought never to have married her. She was never happy with me.'

'But, Jon, you *loved* her!'

Now Jon turned and looked directly at her.

'I thought I did. I really believed I did. She was so beautiful. I think most men who came into her orbit desired her just as I did. But that isn't love.'

Mandy was silent. Jon's words were painfully true to her, too. What she felt for Mike and had tried so hard to call love was no more than Jon had felt for Gillian — an attraction of the senses, and even that was only the faintest stirring of the depths of passion of which she knew herself capable.

'So you decided to divorce Gillian!' she said, bemused.

Jon gave a brief laugh.

'Surely you don't think Gilly would agree to that? She is divorcing me!'

'But on what grounds?'

'Mental cruelty!'

'But that's not possible!' Mandy cried. 'No one could have been more loving, more forgiving, more tolerant. Why . . . ' She broke off, aware of Jon's eyes searching her face. She had spoken so vehemently, so passionately in his defence.

'Does it matter who takes the blame when a marriage breaks up?' he asked rhetorically. 'I don't think so. I don't believe it will greatly affect my practice and as for myself, in a way I am to blame for ever having married her. My only excuse is that I didn't know what real love was until I discovered I loved you.'

Mandy's eyes widened in disbelief. He mistook her expression for one of dismay, for he said quickly:

'I know I shouldn't have said that. You're about to marry the man you love and I'm glad for you and happy that you have found happiness. I never would have told you but for the extraordinary coincidence of running into you, finding you so helpless and distressed. I had to look after you and then, somehow, it just slipped out. Forgive me, Mandy, and forget what I said.'

'Forget it!' Mandy said wildly. 'But I don't want to. I'm in love with you, Jon. I have been for ages and ages. That's why I went away — why I left. I didn't think it was possible to go on living so near you, loving you so much, without you guessing.'

Jon's expression was a mixture of joy and distress.

'But Mike!' he said helplessly. 'You're going to marry Mike!'

She tried to explain, but another thought kept intruding on the explanation, forcing itself to the forefront of her mind until she finally interrupted herself, saying:

'But I don't understand, Jon. If it was Geoff who told Gillian Mike and I were going to be married, Geoff must have known Gillian had left you. And if he knew, Mike must have known. Patty, too. Why didn't they tell me? Why didn't Mike tell me?'

'Because I knew if you ever found out Jon was free, you'd never marry me! I swore Geoff and Patty to secrecy, too.'

Mike stood in the doorway, his face twisted and bitter, his voice hard and matter-of-fact. Then, with a touch of his old flippancy, he said:

'If you'd wanted a private *tête-à-tête* with Jon, my dear Mandy, you should have shut the front door behind you. Needless to say, I couldn't exactly help overhearing your remarks as I came upstairs. Anyway, seeing the truth is out, I suppose I might as well remove myself. Try not to think too badly of me, Mandy. I gambled and lost, but it did seem worth a try.'

'But you knew! You knew I loved Jon. You knew!' Mandy said unbelievingly. 'How could you, Mike?'

He gave a wry smile.

'Because I loved you. I suppose there

are some who might say if I'd really loved you, I'd have put your happiness before my own, but I thought and I still do, that if you'd married me, I could have made you happy. I thought you'd forget Jon in time.'

He gave a long painful sigh.

'I suppose that's it, then. I don't imagine you'll feel much like forgiving me, Mandy, but some day maybe you'll remember me without bitterness. At least, try not to hate me.'

After he had gone Mandy turned to Jon and said:

'Mike must have known I'd find out some time. If I'd heard about your separation from Gillian after I'd married him, then I would truly have hated him. As it is . . . I just don't seem able to feel anything at all.'

'Not even a spark of love for me?' Jon asked, as he put his arms round her.

She lay against him, feeling his lips against her cheek, her heart so full of love that even Timmy was momentarily forgotten.

'I'm so afraid!' she whispered after a moment. 'So afraid this is all a dream and any moment now I'll wake up.'

But as Jon's lips came down on hers she knew with every fibre of her being that she was awake and more alive than she had ever been before.

When finally they broke apart Jon said shakily:

'I almost feel sorry for the poor bloke. He must have loved you pretty desperately, darling. To lose you at the eleventh hour is pretty galling to say the least.'

Mandy touched his cheek with her fingertips, gently tracing the outline of his face.

'Don't let's talk about him. I can't bear to think about it, Jon. If I hadn't run into you at the hospital today, I'd have married him in a fortnight's time. I meant to go through with it, Jon, I really meant to.'

He laughed.

'You make it sound like an ordeal, darling. Surely you must have *wanted* to marry him?'

'But I didn't!' Mandy cried. 'I mean, I wanted to want to, but inside I didn't. Oh, I don't know, Jon, it's all so confused. I was grateful to Mike, and he was so attached to Timmy. Maybe he just paid Timmy so much attention because he knew it would affect me that way. Timmy needs a father and I . . . I needed to forget you, Jon. Somehow, I had to forget you, to stop thinking about you, loving you. I hoped, if I did marry Mike . . . '

'Now we'll never know!' Jon said without a hint of regret in his voice. 'Poor devil! Not that he deserves any sympathy. All the same, my darling, I'm sorry for any man who's lost you. I love you, very, very much. Will you marry me — just as soon as I'm free?'

'You know I will. Jon, darling, hold me again in case I start thinking it's a dream. Hold me tight. Don't ever let me go.'

'Never!' Jon promised. 'For as long as we both shall live.'

We do hope that you have enjoyed reading this large print book.

Did you know that all of our titles are available for purchase?

We publish a wide range of high quality large print books including:
Romances, Mysteries, Classics
General Fiction
Non Fiction and Westerns

Special interest titles available in large print are:
The Little Oxford Dictionary
Music Book, Song Book
Hymn Book, Service Book

Also available from us courtesy of Oxford University Press:
Young Readers' Dictionary
(large print edition)
Young Readers' Thesaurus
(large print edition)

For further information or a free brochure, please contact us at:
Ulverscroft Large Print Books Ltd.,
The Green, Bradgate Road, Anstey,
Leicester, LE7 7FU, England.
Tel: (00 44) 0116 236 4325
Fax: (00 44) 0116 234 0205

THE APOTHECARY'S DAUGHTER

June Davies

Keziah Sephton is kept busy caring for three generations of her family, as well as running the family apothecary shop. George Cunliffe has loved Keziah since they were youngsters, and when Benedict Clay arrives at the shop claiming to be blood kin, and is welcomed into the heart of the family, George is immediately suspicious of the soft-spoken Southern gentleman's motives . . . After her grandmother's precious Book of Hours disappears, Keziah is tormented by treacherous doubts and swiftly enmeshed in a shocking spiral of deception, betrayal, ruthless ambition — and cold-blooded murder.